A DARK RADIANT RAIN

A SAWYER PAYNE AND KACE MASON MYSTERY

MICHAEL LISTER

PULPWOOD PRESS

Books by Michael Lister

(John Jordan Novels)
Power in the Blood
Blood of the Lamb
Flesh and Blood
(Special Introduction by Margaret Coel)
The Body and the Blood
Double Exposure
Blood Sacrifice
Rivers to Blood
Burnt Offerings
Innocent Blood
(Special Introduction by Michael Connelly)
Separation Anxiety
Blood Money
Blood Moon
Thunder Beach
Blood Cries
A Certain Retribution
Blood Oath
Blood Work
Cold Blood
Blood Betrayal
Blood Shot
Blood Ties
Blood Stone

Blood Trail
Bloodshed
Blue Blood
And the Sea Became Blood
The Blood-Dimmed Tide
Blood and Sand
A John Jordan Christmas
Blood Lure
Blood Pathogen
Beneath a Blood-red Sky

(Jimmy Riley Novels)
The Girl Who Said Goodbye
The Girl in the Grave
The Girl at the End of the Long Dark Night
The Girl Who Cried Blood Tears
The Girl Who Blew Up the World

(Merrick McKnight / Reggie Summers Novels)
Thunder Beach
A Certain Retribution
Blood Oath
Blood Shot

(Remington James Novels)
Double Exposure
(includes intro by Michael Connelly)
Separation Anxiety
Blood Shot

(Sam Michaels / Daniel Davis Novels)
Burnt Offerings
Blood Oath
Cold Blood
Blood Shot

For Denise,

Such a gift of solar-powered bliss. You exude the most positive energy in the most magnificent way. Thank you so much for exuding some on me.

PROLOGUE

It was raining the night he disappeared.

An odd, soft rain that refracted the pale, anemic points of light scattered throughout the dark night in irregular and surreal ways, as if everything was taking place in a Dalí painting.

More sheets of mist than isolated and individual drops, the effect was a hazy, hypnotic vibe that seemed to suffuse the wet world entire.

The band worked in all the songs about rain they knew, and by the end of their last set had played CCR's "Have You Ever Seen the Rain," Prince's "Purple Rain," Dylan's "A Hard Rain's A-Gonna Fall," Willie Nelson's "Blue Eyes Crying in the Rain," James Taylor's "Fire and Rain," the Eurythmics' "Here Comes the Rain Again," and the Carpenters' "Rainy Days and Mondays."

It was the kind of night that felt risky, unsteady, and unsafe.

But there was nothing in the atypical atmosphere to portend a young man would so thoroughly and completely vanish off the face of the earth forever.

And yet, that's exactly what happened.

1

Like the three previous nights, Sawyer Payne's eyes open at 4:44 in the morning.

Instantly wide awake.

Fumbling for his phone on the nightstand, he checks for any communications from her. Finding none, as usual and not unexpected, he returns the device to the stack of unread self-help books silently mocking him from their prime position next to where he lays his head these days.

Pushing himself up out of the still unfamiliar bed, he drifts over to the window on his way to the bathroom.

Like so many nights before, he raises the white wooden slats slightly and peers into the dim, foggy semi-darkness, rubbing bits of sleep from the corners of his bleary eyes.

Across the way, in the perfectly manicured micro yards of the too close homes, bright orange plastic jack-o-lanterns flicker as if containing actual candles instead of the bulb of an electric light, fake and meretricious as most of the elements in Forgotten Coast Estates.

The Estates is a massive coastal development, nearly a city unto itself, nestled among the slash pines of North Florida along old Highway 98 in a region once dominated by the timber industry. Until the paper mill, whose acrid smoke smelling of rotten eggs, closed, it served as a repellent for tourists, snowbirds, and high-end planned and gated communities like this one.

What the hell's he doing here?

You know what.

Hiding, of course. Nursing his wounds. Regrouping. Contemplating his as yet undetermined next move. But mostly hiding.

And obsessing.

When he's not obsessing about what went wrong with Jules, he's preoccupied with what happened to Ryan Shandling.

But as baffling as that bizarre disappearance is, he knows it's just a distraction from the disillusionment of his marriage and the healing and recovery work he needs to be doing.

Still, a young man walking into a bar and never walking out again is one of the great unsolved mysteries of our time, and his mind loves working whodunits—especially the more puzzling ones that involve questions of human psychology.

Ryan Shandling, a 27-year-old medical student, was here at the Estates visiting his parents at Halloween two years ago. After begrudgingly helping his dad hand out candy to all the eager little trick-or-treaters so that his mom could attend an out-of-town party with her best friend, he went on a costumed pub-crawl with his on-again off-again friend Tad Roberts.

After several hours and far more shots, the two wound up at Psycho Suzi's, a trying-to-be trendy bar a couple of blocks outside the Estates. Somewhere along the way, Tad had met up with Jennifer Oliver, a sometime girlfriend, who accompanied them to Psycho Suzi's.

Psycho Suzi's is on the second story of an entertainment complex, part of which was under construction at the time. The three are shown riding up the escalator to the bar at 1:15 a.m.

Later, at 1:50 a.m., the same camera shows Ryan standing out in front of the bar on the landing near the escalator talking to two young women. After a few moments, he steps out of frame and back into the bar.

Ryan Shandling is never seen again.

Security cameras cover every entrance and exit of the building. Ryan is clearly shown entering the bar, but never exiting.

Tad and Jennifer, who can be seen leaving via the escalator at 2:01 a.m., claim they both searched for and called Ryan before leaving, but unable to find him and getting no answer, assumed he had left without them. Not only is that something he had done before, but he and Tad had engaged in a drunken argument earlier and had split up sometime around 1:30 a.m.

Now, with the approach of Halloween and the two-year anniversary of Ryan's disappearance, Sawyer thinks he sees someone across the way near the house on the left—Ryan Shandling's mother's house. A dark figure vanishing around the corner in the back.

He just imagined it, right? The result of a foggy night, the approach of Halloween, and thinking of Ryan Shandling.

Has to be.

Still, just in case, he should go check.

"Uncle Sawyer."

He turns to see Addie, his three-year-old niece, who's also living with his mother at the moment.

She's squinting up at him beneath sleep-wild hair and a furrowed brow, a pained expression on her little pale face.

"Have a bad dream?" he asks. "Need to—"

"My skeleton hurts."

He smiles as he bends down to pick her up, charmed as usual by what comes out of her mouth—even when she's feeling poorly.

He doesn't have to kiss her forehead to know she has a fever, but he does it anyway.

"I'm gonna choke," she says.

He leans back a little and looks at her—running toward the restroom with her when he realizes *choke* is Addie for *vomit*.

Before he can reach the restroom she is throwing up on his Jason Isbell No Haters tee.

Clutching her small head, he supports her body as she convulses and begins to cry.

"It's okay," he says. "Just let it out. You'll feel better."

"I want my mommy," she says between heaves.

"I know," he says, his voice full of understanding and pity. Then he tells her the lie that he and his mother keep repeating. "She'll be back soon."

Addie's father is the son of the man Sawyer's mother Robin had been with most recently for a short time. Both Addie's father and mother are drug addicts—and not the casual kind. Though no blood relation, Robin is now raising her as if she is her own, and that's how Sawyer feels about her now—like she's family, his own daughter or granddaughter. More and more he finds himself wishing both her parents would just stay out of her life completely. All they do is call occasionally or drop by unannounced when they want to borrow money—both of which make her anxious and upset and take her days to get over.

Using his sleeve to wipe her mouth and nose, he bends down and turns on the shower.

The vomiting subsided for the moment, she opens her mouth wide and sticks out her tongue, trying not to taste the residue of sickness still present there.

With the water warm, he steps into the shower with her, both of them still fully clothed.

He can't believe how much he's bonded with her during the less than three months that he's lived here, but in many ways she already feels like one of his own, or maybe what a grandchild will feel like—if one his grown children ever get around to giving him that experience.

He has two, a girl and a boy—now a woman and a man—both in their twenties, both doing pretty well, both concerned about their dad, both on their annual Halloween camping trip with their significant others and out of touch for a little while. And though he misses them and their nearly daily interactions, he's happy not to have to answer *How are you doing, Dad? No, really,* several times a day.

"Rinse your mouth out," he says, holding her up to the spray of warm water. "Put water in your mouth and swish it around like this." He demonstrates by actually allowing water into his mouth. "Then spit it out."

She does as he just has.

"Yucky," she says, still trying to keep her tongue from touching the other parts of her mouth.

"Do it again."

She does.

"Better?"

She shakes her head and frowns, her wounded eyes and pitiful face placing a pang at the center of his heart.

He starts to take off his shirt and her PJs, but she clings to him.

"Let's get out of these clothes that have . . . choke on them," he says.

She shakes her head and hugs him tighter.

"Okay," he says, maneuvering them under the warm water. "Let me know when you're ready to take them off. It'll feel better to get them off and get cleaned up. We'll put some fresh clothes on you. And we need to get you some medicine."

"I got boo-boos," she says.

"Yes, you do," he says. "Show me where."

She points to her temple and her little tummy.

"Need Band-Aids," she says.

"Princess Band-Aids?" he asks. "Well, let's get you cleaned up and go get some."

She shakes her head and clings to him even harder.

"You want to sleep with Nana after we get your medicine and Band-Aids?"

"*You-ou-ou*," she says.

His heart feels like it flips up into his throat.

"You got it," he says, amazed again at how quickly they have bonded.

"And watch *Beauty and Beast* on your phone."

"*Ab-so-lutely.*"

Later, cleaned, medicined, and back in bed, Addie propped in the crook of his arm watching *Beauty and the Beast* on his phone, he remembers seeing the figure at the Shandling place.

"I need to borrow my phone to make a quick call, okay?" he says.

"Okay," she says, her voice still weak and raspy.

"Won't take but a second."

He lifts his phone and calls the Estates security—something residents are instructed to do before calling the police. After explaining who he is, he takes an even longer time to explain what he may have seen and why he's bothering them with it.

"We got a lot of calls like this last Halloween too," the soft-spoken dispatcher says. "It's probably nothing, but someone else already called it in, so we're checkin' it out. It's what we're here for. You have yourself a good night . . . and give your mom my best. That's a sweet lady right there now."

Ending the call, he finds Addie fast asleep beside him, and though his arm may be useless tomorrow, he's not about to move her off of it.

2

———————

Kace startles awake in the uncomfortable chair she sleeps in beside his bed, the binder falling from her numb hands to her lap.

After making sure he's still breathing, she glances at the clock on the nightstand. It's 4:44 in the morning.

Yawning, she rubs her tired eyes and stretches, shaking out her fingers to wake up her hands. As is her perpetual state these days, she is stiff and knotted, achy and sore—only more so.

She looks down at the homemade missing persons case binder in her lap—what she thinks of rightly or wrongly as a murder book.

Do detective bureaus have "missing books"?

Doesn't have the same ring to it.

She tries to remember what she had been reading when she drifted off.

With the approach of the second anniversary of Ryan Shandling's disappearance, she is rereading everything she has compiled about the case, which as a former investigative journalist with a touch of obsessive compulsive disorder is a lot.

Former investigative journalist sounds grandiose for what she was. She had been a nurse with an interest in true crime and writing when she became aware of the epidemic of drug-abusing nurses and wrote a multi-part article about it that became a syndicated sensation. The success of that piece gave her the opportunity to investigate and write others, and though none were ever as successful as that first one, she learned a bit about investigating along the way.

Her heart rate rises and she feels a dull, aching nausea low in her abdomen when she thinks about those days. Her long-term live-in boyfriend at the time had been one of the nurses stealing narcotics from the hospital and both selling and abusing them. Her exposé not only ended their relationship, but cost him his career and actually put him in prison. Even though she is hiding in the most unlikely of places, she keeps expecting him to find her and finish the job he had started back when he was on trial and had escalated from stalking and harassing to assault and attempted murder. She's pretty sure he'll kill her one day. Charles had saved her, used his resources to take her away, to bring her here where she is surrounded by people nearly twice her age, but she's always believed it was just delaying the inevitable—especially now that he's dying and Cody's been released.

As usual, when she thinks about Cody she hears The Police's "Every Breath You Take," a song she has come to despise. After she broke things off with him and he began to stalk her, he told her that it was their song and that he would always be watching her.

God, she'd love to solve this case before Cody could get her.

Ryan Shandling's case is never far from her thoughts—it's a great distraction from the dread and sadness she feels and she believes each Halloween that rolls around brings with it heightened opportunities to discover what really happened to Ryan and who's responsible for his disappearance.

She remembers now. She had been reading a printout of a lengthy subreddit on Ryan's complicated and conflicted relationship with Tad Roberts.

The two young men had never been especially close, and it seems as if nearly every encounter ended in an argument, but for some reason they had continued to hang out occasionally over the years.

She's very suspicious of the frenemy who not only peppered his early statements to the police and media with subtle and not so subtle criticisms of Ryan but also quickly lawyered up and refused to take a polygraph—the only person asked by authorities to do so.

Tad's not the only one she's suspicious of and has seemingly endless questions for. She finds the entire case nearly as perplexing as Maura Murray, JonBenét Ramsey, and Abby Williams and Liberty Rose Lynn German. But she can't help but believe that she could solve it if she wasn't so mentally, emotionally, and physically fatigued all the time.

Not that she's complaining.

Caring for Charles has given her more purpose than she's ever had and has called forth the very best of her. Charles had saved her from Cody, had offered her safety and security and a rebirth of sorts, but then she had saved him, saved his literal life so many times since then. How could she not feel that her previous career had prepared her for this moment, this most critical of assignments? She's not only excelling as a nurse-wife, but as a human being—one focused on what really matters in life, with no time for the trivial, transient concerns that seem to occupy the time and energy of so many. These days it's a truly rare occurrence for her to care what anyone thinks of her or for her to care in any kind of petty or judgmental way what they get up to.

And that's so different from when they first got together—when she wasted way, way too much time caring about people's opinions of her and her husband who was old enough to be her father. She not only obsessed about others' opinions, but expended far too much energy in the fear of missing out, of being left out—which she was. A lot. He was too old for her friend group. She was too young for his. Ironically, she felt far more lonely and isolated back then than these days when she rarely ever sees another human being besides him—and nearly never a friend.

With as much time as he sleeps, she has never been more alone in her life, yet she's never felt less lonely. His extended illness hasn't just transformed him. In many ways the greatest changes have taken place within her. *His* cancer has caused *her* metamorphosis.

And part of that alteration is a seasoned and secure sense of self-confidence, which among many other things convinces her she can solve Ryan's case, given the bandwidth to actually work it.

But, she thinks as she stands and stretches, she hopes that's something she never gets—*that would mean Charles dying.*

Or, another voice inside her says—the one she thinks of as Positive Patti—*full remission and recovery.*

Wouldn't it be pretty to think so.

The symptoms of Charles's particular brand of lymphoma wax and wane. He's been in a cycle of getting better for a little while and then worse, better and worse, but she fears he won't get better this time. He hasn't responded too well to any treatments they've tried, and his condition at any given time is completely unpredictable and capricious.

As she wanders over to the window, her eyes widen in surprise to see through the fog and beyond the false flicker of plastic jack-o-lanterns a fellow insomniac gazing into the same dark abyss of night that she is.

The curve of the cul-de-sac, her home's position near the

mouth of it, and the slight incline it's on give her a great view of both the houses in it and the ones leading up to it.

If she's not mistaken, it's Robin Shaw's son, the relationships guy.

Wonder if this is when he gets his ideas and insights.

Suddenly, he looks alarmed, and she follows his distressed stare over toward Sheri Shandling's house.

For an instant she thinks she sees a dark figure disappearing around the far side, but surely that's just her—

Charles begins to choke, and she turns from the window and rushes over to the home hospital bed that has replaced their California King.

3

Sawyer looks up to see the reflection of blue lights flashing on the ceiling.

Carefully lifting Addie's head with his free hand, he slowly extricates his arm and gently transfers her to a pillow.

Easing out of bed, he rushes over to the window to see an Estates security vehicle in front of Sheri Shandling's place.

Glancing back at Addie and seeing she is sleeping soundly, he decides to get dressed, set up the baby monitor, and go get a closer look.

He throws on jeans and a Beatles tee and moves the baby monitor system from Addie's room to his. Less than five minutes later, he is crossing the cul-de-sac, the soft, sweet sounds of Addie's breathing coming through the small speaker of the battery-powered portable baby monitor in his hand.

He arrives at the scene at the same time as an auburn-haired woman who looks to be a bit younger than him—something unicorn-uncommon in this restricted retirement community. Her green eyes seems to glow in the flashing lights, and her skin is so pale as to look ghostly.

Like him, she must be visiting her parents. Probably

brought her kids for the big Halloween extravaganza. Of course, unless she got a very late start, her kids would be too old for that, and unless she got a very early start, she wouldn't have grandkids old enough for it.

He's shocked to see she too is carrying a baby monitor in her hand.

Smiling, they each raise their monitors by way of greeting.

Beyond the new bright, shiny, white security vehicle, a petite boyish-looking officer is still knocking on the front door. Getting no response, he bangs harder.

A moment later, another officer with a flashlight walks around from the back to join him. She is tall and thin and towers over her preteen-looking partner.

"She's probably sound asleep, the poor thing," she says. "No sign of anything back there. Nothing out of place. Nothing disturbed. No sign of a break-in."

"That's 'cause we don't have break-ins in the Estates," he says, and Sawyer can't tell whether he's being sarcastic or not.

Turning toward Sawyer and the woman watching them, the tall female security officer says, "Everything's all right folks. We're just doing a welfare check on this residence. Y'all go on back to your homes. We got this."

Neither of them move.

Sawyer glances over at the auburn-haired woman not far from him, and they exchange knowing, amused reactions.

And then his eyes do something they haven't done in a very long time—they drift down to her left hand in search of a ring.

What're you doing? No. Uh huh. Absolutely not. Stop it. Don't even think about it. Your divorce isn't even final yet, and you—

I didn't mean— It was just— I did it before I realized what I was doing.

You swore you were going to be alone for a while.

I am.

Heal. Address some issues. Regroup so you don't repeat the same tired old mistakes.

No question. I just— I'm not sure why I did it. I didn't mean to. Won't happen again.

Make sure it doesn't.

But as he follows her gaze back toward the security officers, he's filled with a warm, subtle sensation that could only be described as pleasurable.

Before he realizes what he's doing, he steps over to her.

"I called them," he says.

"Me too."

"Thought I saw a dark figure running around to the back of her house."

"Me too."

"I'm glad to hear you say that. Thought I might have been imagining it . . . With Halloween and the anniversary of Ryan's disappearance."

She comes to a full stop and turns to take him in more carefully.

"I had the same thought," she says. "Most people around here don't speak about it so directly."

"Probably would've thought of it anyway," he says. "Been reading up on the case a lot lately. I'm a— I used to be a police psychologist and I'm a bit of an amateur forensics psychologist. But the fact that he was near Ryan's mom's house . . ."

"Or she," she says. "Figure I saw could've been a man or a woman."

He nods. "True. You're right. I shouldn't've said—"

"I'm Kace, by the way," she says. "I see you looking out your bedroom window some nights. The street lamp creates cool shadows on you from the blinds."

"Cool name," he says. "I'm—

"You're the Your Love Guru dot com guy, aren't you?"

He had always been embarrassed by the domain his

publisher had secured for his blog, but now it was mortifying. And not just because of his breakup.

"The name my mother gave me is Sawyer," he says.

"Nothing wrong with that, but . . . doesn't quite have the ring of Your Love Guru dot com."

It was actually Your Love And Relationship dot com, which only makes it worse, and he doesn't mention it.

"Your mother is Robin, right? Think I saw you staring out the window earlier."

He nods. "That's when I saw him. Or thought I did. Which house are you—"

She turns and points to a house two lots down, which because of the curve of the cul-de-sac is set back a bit.

"So you can see into her backyard?"

"A little," she says. "Looked like he or she was in all black and maybe . . . had a . . . cape."

"I thought I saw one too, but wasn't going to mention that."

"Surely someone who goes by Your Love Guru dot com isn't embarrassed by admitting he saw a cape on a cat burglar."

"I don't *go* by it," he says. "I didn't have anything to do with it."

"So you're not the Your Love Guru dot com?"

"You realize you don't have to add *dot com* every time, don't you? You don't have to say any of it at all."

"Fine, but are you or are you not the Your Love Guru dot com? I need to know. What if I have a question or wake up in need of some guru-ing . . . Be good to know that Your Love Guru dot com is right here in the same cul-de-sac."

Before he can respond, his phone vibrates in his pocket. Shocked someone is calling at five-something in the morning, he snatches it out and looks at it. It's his mom.

"Where are you?" she asks. "Sheri just called and said someone's in her house."

4

As Sawyer runs toward the back of the house, he hears glass shattering and takes off in an all out sprint. Both Kace and the female security officer following him, can't keep up.

"Hey, stop," the security officer yells. "Estates Security. Freeze. Now."

He continues running, wondering if the female officer is fast enough to catch up to him and either tackle or tase him.

"He's not the bad guy," Kace yells. "He's Your Love Guru dot com."

Running through Sheri's lush flower garden, he stumbles over a planter and knocks over an old painted bicycle, but keeps moving.

His mom had told him where the key to Sheri's backdoor was hidden, but as he reaches the little patio he sees it won't be necessary.

Beyond the little outdoor table and a few ficus plants, one side of the white French doors is wide open, its jam splintered, the striker plate dangling down.

"I just checked this," the security officer says. "It was locked up securely."

Sawyer only slows a little as he enters the dark house.

Kace and the security officer follow more slowly, cautiously, the latter pulling out her taser.

"Sheri," Sawyer yells. "It's Robin's son, Sawyer. The Estates security is here too. Where are you? Are you okay? Is anyone in here with you?"

"In the bedroom," Sheri yells. "I'm alone."

He rushes over to the bedroom as someone behind him turns on a light.

"Sir, wait for me," the security officer says. "Let me—"

Ignoring her, Sawyer runs into the room.

He finds Sheri Shandling frozen in fear, hiding beneath the covers like a frightened child, face red and glistening, eyes wide and wild, out of breath and coughing.

"You're okay now," he says. "We're here. Are you hurt?"

"Just my pride," she says, peeking out from the covers. "Never been so scared in all my life. Didn't handle it particularly well."

"What happened?"

"I woke up with someone on top of me," she says.

She makes a move to come out from beneath the covers and Sawyer offers his hand to help her sit up.

"Thank you," she says.

Like his mom, Sheri is trim and fit and has a youthful bearing. Beneath her modern, stylish, short blond hair, her pampered face shows only the finest lines and slightest looseness of skin. Even in her disheveled and frightened state she is attractive and appears at least a decade younger than she really is.

Kace comes back into the room with two glasses, joining Sawyer and the security person crowding in beside Sheri's bed.

"Brandy or water?" she asks, holding them up.

"Brandy, please. Thank you, dear."

Sheri sips the brandy.

If she is self-conscious about having her hair taped up on her head, no makeup on her face, or the outlines of her breasts showing through her thin navy-blue nightgown, she doesn't show it.

"He was holding me down. I woke up with someone holding me down—sitting on my stomach, pinning my arms to the bed. Told me not to be afraid, he wasn't here to hurt me, but . . . Said he was my Ryan, but I know it wasn't. Ryan would never do something like that to me. He knows I have a weak heart. He was whispering. Hard to hear and understand, but . . . the way he called me *Mom* . . . It wasn't him. I just know it."

Sawyer tries to recall the size and shape of the figure he had seen. He had only had eyes on him for a moment. He thinks maybe he could've been tall enough to be Ryan, but he can't be sure. He was crouched and running and in all black in the darkness. But if it was Ryan, he has lost a lot of weight since he's been missing.

"Did he say anything else?" the security officer asks.

She nods, takes another sip of her brandy. "Said he was healthy and happy and to stop looking for him. Just let him live his life in the peace it took him so long to find. And then he climbed off me. He said something else as he was leaving but I didn't make it out. That was it. Didn't hurt me—well, besides my wrists a little."

She rubs her right wrist with her left hand, then sets her brandy down on the bedside table and rubs her left wrist with her right hand.

"I'm so glad you're okay," Kace says. "I better get back to Charles but don't hesitate to call me if I can do anything."

"Thank you, dear, but you have more than enough on you. I'm fine. Thank you for coming to my rescue."

"That was all him," she says, nodding toward Sawyer. "I was just an also-ran and bartender."

Sawyer turns to say something to Kace, but she's already through the door.

Turning back to Sheri, he says, "I know Mom would say you're staying with us tonight and she wouldn't take *no* for an answer."

"Wouldn't dream of giving one. No way I'm staying here."

"We're going to do a thorough search of the place and call in the sheriff's department," the officer says, "but we can wait until tomorrow to take your statement."

"You poor thing," Robin is saying. "How awful. It's just unbelievable. *Here.*"

The Estates are marketed as the safest community in Florida, and it's a big part of the attraction to retirees who flock here—particularly the divorced and widowed women who live alone.

The three of them—Sheri, Robin, and Sawyer—are sitting at Robin's dining table having a cup of Sleepytime tea—and though Addie's not far away and the door to the guest room where she's still sleeping is ajar, the baby monitor sits on the table in front of him.

"Maybe it's not as safe here as we think it is," Robin says. "Or as it used to be."

Even in the middle of the night, Robin looks regal—a result of both her bearing and her beauty. She has dark, shortish hair that doesn't appear dyed, and dark, penetrating eyes, the lids of which don't sag down to obscure them. His entire life he has been told how beautiful his mother is, and at her age in the middle of the night with no makeup on, it's easy to see why.

Sheri shakes her head. "Pretty sure it's isolated to me. Has everything to do with what happened to my Ryan. And that happened off the Estates."

"Yeah, but just barely," Robin says. "And what happened tonight didn't."

"But it's only because of the other."

"Did he have a weapon?" Robin asks.

"Not that I saw."

"And he said he was Ryan."

"Yeah, but he wasn't," Sheri says. "A mother knows her son —two years later or twenty years later. It wasn't him."

Robin nods, glancing at her own son as she does. "That's true. So true."

"Mothers have special connections to their children," Sheri says. "I'd know if Ryan were dead. I'd feel it in my womb. I know he's still out there somewhere. And I'd have known if that was him tonight—even with him whispering in the dark with a mask on."

He doesn't doubt the connection between mother and child, but he knows a lot of mothers who were convinced their children were still alive right up until and sometimes even after their dead bodies were discovered.

She hadn't mentioned a mask. "What kind of mask was it?" he asks.

She shakes her head. "I'm not sure. It was dark. And to be honest I had my eyes closed much of the time."

"You didn't see it?" he asks.

She shakes her head.

"Did you feel it?" he asks. "Touch it, or did he graze across your skin at any point?"

"No. Sorry."

"What about smell?" he asks. "What did it smell like?"

Her eyes widen. "Oh, wow, it did smell . . . Kind of . . . rubbery."

"Could it have been latex?" he asks. "Like a Halloween mask."

Her eyes widen again, accompanied by her mouth opening this time, and she begins to nod—slowly at first. "Yes," she says. "Has to be. That's it. But . . . why wear a Halloween mask if he wanted me to know it was him?"

"Good, isn't he?" Robin says, nodding at Sawyer. "Given enough time and information, I think he can solve the case and find Ryan."

As much as he'd like to do exactly that, he wishes she wouldn't say things like that—particularly to the mother of the missing man.

But given Sheri's lack of reaction, he's not sure it even registered with her.

She's still gazing up and off into the distance. "It's just so bizarre. A Halloween mask."

"Ryan did go missing on Halloween," Robin says.

"Kace and I both thought he was wearing a cape too," he says.

"It's downright surreal," Sheri says. "I mean . . . beyond being unimaginably cruel . . . it's just strange."

"Wonder if it's the same person who posted on the funeral home website," Robin says.

Less than two short months after Ryan vanished, his dad, Philip, had fallen from the attic while retrieving Christmas decorations. Crashing through insulation and the ceiling to land on the hallway floor, he had seemed fine at the time—just bruised and sore once the wind that had been knocked out of him returned. But three days later he died suddenly of a delayed aortic dissection—the trauma from the fall causing a small tear in his aorta that went undetected. His injury caused no real pain or cause for concern, and then without warning his injured aorta gave way and ruptured.

The funeral home providing his burial services had an

online guestbook for friends and family to sign who couldn't attend the memorial service. One of the entries read: Miss you, Dad. See you soon. Love, your son, Ryan (the Virgin Islands).

"Anyone capable of that kind of cruelty could certainly do something like this," Robin adds.

"I'm not convinced that wasn't Ryan who signed the book," Sheri says. "I know what the cops say, but . . . just because he wasn't really in the Virgin Islands doesn't mean it wasn't him. But I know for a fact that guy tonight wasn't."

She's right. Just because the authorities discovered that the IP address used to send the message to the virtual guestbook was a local internet cafe and not somewhere in the Virgin Islands doesn't mean it wasn't Ryan. If he really did walk out of his life like some theorize, he'd pick a place as far away as he could to sign in from. It was odd to include a place in parentheses like that anyway. No one else did.

5

———————

There is no crime scene tape on or police presence at Sheri Shandling's house. Nor did Sawyer expect there to be. Homes didn't get broken into in the Estates. It didn't fit the narrative of the safest community in Florida. He wonders if they even reported it to the sheriff's department.

It's midmorning the next day, the October sun high overhead serving as the centerpiece of a clear blue sky. It's still North Florida warm, but mercifully the humidity level has dropped to a more pleasing percentage.

Sawyer is ostensibly walking over to grab some things for Sheri, but the real reason for his return visit is to get a better look at the crime scene without security looking at him.

Though Sheri has given him a key to the front door, he walks around back to enter the broken French doors of the patio, wanting to see them and the backyard in daylight.

Like many of the homes in the Estates, Sheri's postage stamp lot backs up to the fairway of one of the many holes of the excessive golf courses that weave in and out and around and through every other element of the Estates.

The Estates-provided barrier between Sheri's few feet of

yard and the golf course is made up of planted palms, flowering shrubs, perennials, and annuals that follow the curve of the sand traps on this side. But the real barrier is Sheri's elaborate and verdant flower garden—something that violates the strict Estates covenants and is under constant threat of being forcibly removed.

The outward opening French doors aren't even closed, let alone locked. The busted one is touching the other, but not connected, the hardware not engaged.

He turns his head slightly and glances around furtively to make sure no one is watching him.

Filled with a deep sense of imposter syndrome, he withdraws a latex glove from his pocket and awkwardly slips it on his right hand, opens the broken door, and examines the inside edge where it connects to the other door.

The door on the right appears to be untouched, undamaged. The one on the left, the open one, is splintered above and below the handle mechanism, its inside face near the tempered glass bearing a partial boot print, presumably from where the assailant kicked the door open on his way out.

Examining the hardware, hinges, and lock stile, he doesn't think it would take much force to kick it open. Sheri, like most of the residents, is counting on the Estates and not her own locks to protect her.

After wiping his shoes on the mat to prevent further contamination of the crime scene, Sawyer enters the small house and begins looking around, wondering how long he has before Sheri will begin to suspect he's doing more than having a difficult time finding the items she sent him for.

Like his mom's own home, Sheri's house smells good. And it's immaculate. Everything is in its place and every place is pristine clean. The feminine furniture appears new, and it's obviously expensive without being extravagant. The walls and tabletops are peppered with framed photographs of Ryan and his father, but there are very few pictures of the three of them.

Sheri lost her only child and her husband within two months two years ago. She became a widow and an— Not an orphan. What is the name for a parent who loses a child?

He can't come up with anything and concludes that there isn't a name—probably because such an experience shouldn't exist to need a name.

The floor plan of the little cookie cutter box on the hillside is a master suite on one side, two bedrooms with a Jack and Jill bathroom between them on the other, and an open-concept living room, dining room, and kitchen between them.

When they built, Phil and Sheri added a few features to customize their particular little cookie cutter ticky tacky box, but none more elaborate and dramatic than the white stone fireplace. They probably have to run the air-conditioning in order to use it even a few times a year, but it would be worth it. It, like nearly every other surface of the house, is decorated with pictures of Ryan, including one in a Halloween costume from his last night. It was snapped in front of the house as he and his dad passed out candy, but Sheri has folded it so that Phil was cropped out. As with some of the other photos, it is strategically placed to cover flaws and deep gouges in the unique stone.

He crosses the little living room and opens the first of the two doors to find a standard if overly furnished guest room.

Turning and opening the other door directly behind him, he finds a shrine of sorts to Ryan in the room that presumably has been left much as it was the last time he stayed in it—only now with the addition of items from his dorm room.

Making his way between the dining room table and kitchen island, he stops at the entryway to the master suite and examines the door.

It bears no marks of violence, no signs of forced entry. He'll have to ask her if it had been open or unlocked.

This thought leads to another, and he rushes into the suite to check the bedroom and bathroom windows.

Finding them securely fastened with no signs of damage, he jogs back out of the suite, past the kitchen, and down a little hallway to the front door. From there, he steps over and studies the door connecting the two-car garage, and then past the burgundy Honda Pilot to the garage door itself.

As he starts back into the house from the garage, he thinks he hears someone inside. Quickly scanning the garage, he finds a piece of galvanized pipe with an elbow attached to it in a plastic milk crate of random home repair detritus.

With his left arm out in front of him defensively, he lifts the pipe in his right, pulling it back like the weapon it is, and enters the house again.

6

____

He's only taken two steps inside when the jolt hits him.

Every muscle in his body seizes up, clenching like the worst Charlie horses ever—everywhere simultaneously. He involuntarily releases the length of galvanized pipe and it clatters on the tile of the hallway, landing just moments before he does.

"Oh, no, Sawyer!" Kace yells. "I thought you were the— Are you okay?"

He looks up to see her holding a baby monitor in one hand and a little pink taser in the other.

As his muscles begin to unclench, shudders run the length of his body and he feels the odd and unnatural sensation of having been a conduit for electrical current.

"Wow," she says, holding up her taser and looking at it admiringly, "this little thing really works."

"I'm so glad you're pleased," he says, his voice slow and heavy with sarcasm. "My perspective is a little different."

"I rarely post reviews on stuff, but I think—"

As he tries to stand, his muscles seize up again and he falls back down. When he hits the floor, he tries to bounce right back up—but with the same result. And evidently he looks hilarious doing it because she begins laughing so hard he thinks she might wet herself.

"Stop, stop," she says. "I can't . . . I'm gonna wet myself. Let me help you."

"You've done enough, really," he says.

Placing the taser and monitor on the floor, she leans down and helps lift him up.

A moment after he's upright, his legs cramp up again, but instead of falling down, he falls into her and she holds him up.

"Just relax," she says. "Don't move. Give them a minute."

Two virtual strangers, one having just tased the other, locked in an intimate embrace.

Suddenly, he is self-conscious and embarrassed. Does he smell? He hasn't showered yet today. Of course, he had a partial one at a little before five this morning. Probably smells of vomit.

Their eyes meet, and he's tempted to look away but doesn't.

"Sorry," she says.

"For what?"

She shoots him a quizzical look. "For tasing you."

"Oh. Thanks. What are you doing here?"

"Trying to figure out who broke in, how, and why," she says. "See if it's connected to Ryan's disappearance. You?"

"Same. Plus grabbing Sheri a few things."

"Here's a question for you," she says. "The guy broke out the back door when he heard the security officers knocking, right?" They're now assuming it was a man, based on Sheri's account. "So where'd he break in?"

"He didn't. I just checked all the doors and windows. He didn't break in any of them."

"What does that— Did he have a key? Was it Ryan after all?"

"Good questions," he says. "He may have had a key—and that may tell us who he is. Sheri may have left a door or window open or unlocked. Or he may have gotten in another way."

"Such as?"

"I think I can stand on my own now," he says. "Thanks for holding me up."

She releases him but keeps her hands nearby.

He stands on his own, but places a hand on the wall to support himself.

"Got it?" she says.

He nods. "Thanks. There are a lot of possibilities."

"I only see two," she says. "Me catching you or you hitting the floor again."

"About how he could've gotten in," he says. "He could be somebody she knows who could've come by for a social visit and unlocked a door or window while he was here. Or he could have come on an official visit—a maintenance or repair person of some kind—and done the same thing."

"I can think of another," she says. "Remember the break-in?"

Approximately two months after Ryan went missing and just after her husband's death, Sheri's house was broken into. The investigation conducted by both the Estates security and the Creek County Sheriff's Department concluded that the break-in was unrelated to Ryan's disappearance. It was the holidays and there were a string of burglaries in the wider area, and it appeared that only a few presents and electronics were taken from her home. Sheri's place was the only one in her neighborhood hit by the thieves, which made the authorities take a closer look at it than they might otherwise have, but ultimately they determined that she may have been targeted because she was a single older woman whose son had vanished and whose husband had recently died in a tragic accident.

"What if it really was connected to Ryan's disappearance?" she says. "What if whoever it was took a spare key while he or she was in here?"

He nods. "We need to ask Sheri if all her keys are accounted for."

"Then there's the possibility that it actually was Ryan," she says. "He has a key."

"True. And it's at least possible."

"So if he had a key or a way in of some sort," she says, "why not use it on his way out?"

"Another great question. I don't know. Maybe he was in a hurry and wanted to make his escape through the golf course. Or maybe he wanted us to think that he didn't have a key and—"

"Didn't count on such elite minds working the case?" she offers.

He laughs. "Exactly."

"You okay now?" she asks. "I need to get back."

He nods.

"Prove it," she says.

"How?" he asks, curious what he can do to prove to her he's not going down again.

"Walk me out."

He nods and gestures for her to go first. "Lead the way."

She does, walking faster than he is capable of, though she's not walking in any way that would be considered briskly.

When the gap between them has increased to ten feet, she looks over her shoulder and yells, though it's not necessary, "You okay back there?"

"I'm fine," he says. "I'm going to catch up and overtake you any moment now."

"Good to have goals," she says. "Even absurdly unrealistic ones, I guess."

Though she only reaches the back patio a few seconds

before him, when he steps through the busted door she says, "I was just about to leave you a note."

He starts to say something, but golf course maintenance men working on the sand trap catch his eye.

"Wonder what they're doing," he says. "There's every chance he ran through there as he was making his escape."

"You should go see," she says. "Though what are the chances they'll still be around by the time you can get there?"

He shakes his and lets out a little laugh that is more appreciative than anything else.

"I've got to get back, but let me know if you find out anything." She takes a few steps away, then turns and says, "Sorry again about tasing you."

"No you're not."

"Did provide me with the best laugh I've had in a long time."

"That's all that matters."

She continues walking away.

He watches for a moment then calls after her. "I've always believed that if you're going to give a sorry-not-sorry apology, you might as well not apologize."

Without stopping or even looking back, she nods and says, "Pearls . . . from Your Love Guru dot com."

He watches her for another moment, then sets off toward the golf course.

The longer he walks, the better he gets at it, and by the time he nears the fairway he's nearly moving normally.

As he approaches the sand trap, he sees that the two men in the green Estates sports shirts and khaki shorts are digging something out of it.

He reaches them in time to see one of them hold up a black Halloween costume with the small sand trap rake.

It's a black robe with a hood and cape, a dusting of pure white sand covering it.

As the other one reaches down for the mask, Sawyer says, "Wait. Don't touch it."

"Huh?"

"There was a break-in last night and I think this is what the guy was wearing."

"*Really*?" the one leaning over the mask says, and they both begin to look at the items with awe and appreciation.

"We need to call the Creek County Sheriff's Department and have them come out for it."

"We have to call Estates security," the one holding the costume with the rake says. "They call the sheriff."

"Okay," Sawyer says. "Just get some pictures and be sure not to touch anything."

Without waiting for them to respond, he steps forward and begins to take pictures of his own.

The mask is that of a plain, white, expressionless face, disturbing because of its emptiness, creepy in its inhumanity.

8

7

"We appreciate you calling us," Rick Carson is saying.

He's an investigator with the Creek County Sheriff's Department, and he's sitting in Robin's living room with Sheri and Sawyer. Robin and Addie wander in and out occasionally.

After taking pictures of the costume, Sawyer had called the sheriff's department on his way back, doubtful the Estates security would.

"You'd be surprised at how often incidents and even crimes that happen here in the Estates aren't reported to us," Rick says.

He's a youngish, heavyset white man with short, side-parted blondish hair and a gentleness not often associated with law enforcement.

"Were y'all notified of the break-in to her house last night?" Sawyer asks.

"That's a perfect example," he says. "We weren't."

"That's . . ." Sheri says, "outrageous."

"The Estates is a very safe place to live," Rick says, "but those who own and operate it are trying to sell the notion that it's the safest place on the planet, so they tend to try to suppress anything that contradicts that."

"Well," Sawyer says, "it's doing the residents a real disservice."

"They absolutely are," Rick says. "It's true that most of the time it's related to theft and drunk and disorderly, but occasionally it's related to very serious crimes like assault, rape, maybe even murder."

Sheri shakes her head and lets out a long, heavy sigh.

Robin, who must have occupied Addie with an art project in her room, brings in a tray with glasses of iced tea and a plate of store-bought shortbread cookies and sets it down on the coffee table between them.

They thank her and each take a glass. Rick Carson is the only one to take a cookie, and he takes three.

"You mind taking me through what happened last night?" Rick asks Sheri around a crunchy, crumbly bite of his cookie.

"I was sound asleep and suddenly someone was on top of me, pressing me down, pinning my arms to the bed, covering my mouth. It was very dim, but the nightlight in the bathroom kept it from being pitch black. He had on a mask."

"Like this?" Sawyer asks, holding up his phone to show her the picture of the mask in the sand trap.

"I'll need to get those from you," Rick says.

Sheri nods. "Yes. I think so. I closed my eyes and . . . I was so scared. He whispered some stuff. It was hard to hear. I didn't make out some of it. But it was something like 'Mom, it's me. I'm okay. I just wanted you to know not to worry about me.' Some other stuff I didn't understand. 'I'm playing in a band. I'm happy. Please don't look for me anymore. I'll be in touch.' There was a banging on the front door and he was gone."

"Do you believe it was your son?" Ricks asks.

Sheri is shaking her head before he finishes the question. "I know it wasn't. A mother knows. I know he's still alive, but I also know that wasn't him."

"Did he have any distinguishing . . . *anything*?" Risk asks. "Smells, mannerisms, ticks, accent, speech patterns, movements? Anything."

"No," she says. "At least I don't think so. I really didn't . . . My eyes were closed. I was so scared. I'm afraid I'm a terrible witness."

"Not at all," Rick says.

"Do you mind if I ask . . ." Sawyer says, looking from Rick to Sheri. "Any idea how he got in?"

She looks confused. "Broke in the back patio door."

"Actually, that's where he broke out," he says, and explains to them what he and Kace had discovered and theorized about the assailant's entry into and exit from the house.

"That's very interesting," Rick says. "I'll have to take a look at that."

"I just assume he broke in," Sheri says. "If he didn't . . . I have no idea how he—"

Sawyer says, "Anyone been in recently to do any work for you or repair anything?"

She thinks about it, then shakes her head. "Don't think so."

"Who all has a key?" Sawyer asks, wondering if Rick minds that he's asking so many questions.

"No one that would do anything like that," she says.

Rick says, "I'm sure not, but we need to check with them. Make sure they still have them."

"I'd have to think about it," she says. "I can make you a list. A couple of neighbors for when I go on vacation." She turns to Sawyer. "Your mom has one. Ah . . . Let's see who else . . . My cleaning lady. Ryan has one, of course. And Amy. A few others. I'll—"

"Ryan's ex-girlfriend Amy?" Rick asks.

"I assume she still has one," she says. "I never got it back from her. And she's not his ex."

"Didn't she get engaged recently?"

"Well, yes, but I just . . . Only because she believes Ryan is dead. But I just meant . . . they didn't break up."

"Okay," Rick says. "Sure, I . . . I know what you mean. But yes, if you could make me a list of everyone who has ever had a key . . ."

"I'll do it today . . . as long as you promise not to harass them."

"I promise, ma'am," he says. "That's not how I— That's not my style."

"I have to say this," she says. "I was scared. It was a frightening experience, but . . . I was never in any real danger. Whoever it was didn't intend me any harm. I could tell."

8

____

"I appreciate you calling me," Rick Carson is saying, "more than you know. And the pictures of the costume and mask are . . . they help a lot. I realize the . . . Ryan's disappearance took place outside of the Estates . . . but *just* outside. And Ryan was staying here. As were Tad and Jennifer, so there's an obvious connection even if it's not direct, but the Estates won't cooperate. Who knows, we may have had this thing solved already if they would just assist us—or at least not obstruct us."

Sawyer and Rick are standing out in Robin's small yard in the early afternoon.

"I'm so . . . It's . . . This case is baffling enough without them handicapping me. Two years and not so much as a single solid clue. The media acts like we don't care or that we're just bumbling idiots, but . . . you can't imagine the pressure I feel. Nobody—except Ryan's mom—wants to find him more than I do."

Sawyer nods and gives him a sympathetic look. "It's obvious you care very deeply."

"I do," he says. "I feel so bad for Mrs. Shandling and poor

Amy. I know people say she moved on awfully fast, but I saw how heartbroken she was. She was so in love with him. I think she was expecting to get proposed to on their vacation that next week. Anyway . . . I'm not too proud to ask for help. That insight you had about the break-in last night . . . that was good."

"I wasn't the only one who had it," he says. "Kace Mason who lives over there came to the same conclusion."

"Your mom says you've assisted the police before."

He nods, though he feels a little guilty doing so. "Some," he says.

The truth is, in his private practice he had some police officers, detectives, and deputies for clients because of his contract with the city and county, and on a few occasions, very unofficially, they had asked his opinion on certain aspects of some of his cases. He had found it immensely rewarding and had added study of investigative techniques to his pursuit of forensic psychology and his consumption of all things true crime.

"I don't know how long you'll be visiting your mom, but I'd appreciate any help you'd be willing to give on this case. It'd really help having someone here in the Estates. You would be able to get so much more information than I would. You'll hear things. See things. Make connections. Be able to ask questions. It would have to be just between us. My boss would never go for anything like this, but if you're willing . . ."

"I'd be happy to," he says, thinking about how much it would help to have something to focus on, even obsess over, right now. "And I think we should include Kace Mason if she's going to be around. She's done a lot of work on the case already and—"

"It would just have to be super secretive, and the more people involved, the more chances there are for it to get out, but if you think she'd be good then ask her about it. Just make sure she knows to keep it quiet."

"I will. She will."

"Thing is . . . more and more I'm being pulled off this case for other more immediate ones. It's not getting the attention I want to give it, and my supervisor's not amenable to my requests to spend more time on it. I could really use some help and I think you'd be great."

"So since there's little doubt that what happened last night is related to what happened on Halloween two years ago," Sawyer says, "could you get me up to speed on Ryan's disappearance?"

"I can start," he says. "There's a lot to it and it'd probably be best to talk about it while doing a walkthrough of Suzi's, but . . . essentially all entrances and exits were covered by cameras. Ryan can be seen walking in with Tad Roberts and Jennifer Oliver and he can be seen a little before closing time talking to two girls out front, but as they leave he heads back into the bar, and he is never seen leaving. We searched every inch of that bar and the building it's in. We watched every second of all the video footage from that night—over and over again. We got the surveillance footage from all the nearby businesses. We've looked at all of it. He's not on any of it. It's the most . . . He went into the bar. We know that. He never came out of the bar. We know that. He's not still in the bar. We know that. That's all we know. We haven't gotten anywhere really. There are all sorts of wild theories and crazy speculation online, and we get bizarre tips but it's all garbage—just bored people playing cyber Sherlock."

Sort of like I'm doing, Sawyer thinks.

"I know people are frustrated with us," Rick says. "But there's only one case like this in the history of missing persons. *One*. It's the most baffling missing persons case ever. And it's not unsolved for lack of effort. I've worked my ass off on it. And not just me. And I know we're a small department, but we've had investigators from several other agencies consult on this. It's on me because it's my case, but the best and brightest haven't been able to solve it either."

WHEN SAWYER WALKS BACK into the house, Sheri has packed up her things and is about to return home.

"I really think you should stay here until we can figure out what's going on," he says.

As she stands there holding her small bag, he is struck by how much thinner she is than his mom. She's very tall, which may account for it, but he's heard there's a diet pill epidemic in the Estates and wonders if she has fallen prey to it. Of course, she could've just stopped eating out of grief.

"I appreciate that," she says. "I do, but . . . what if I'm wrong and it *was* Ryan? And even if it wasn't . . . the reason I'm still in that house—even after I've been offered a small fortune for it— is in case Ryan comes home. I want to be there when he comes home."

It's common for families of the missing to refuse to move or change anything—their address, their phone numbers, anything—as a desperate act of faith that their loved one might just return to them one day. The golf course wanted to expand and had offered her up to triple the market value of her home, but she had steadfastly refused. Many residents in the Estates, including Sawyer's mom, believed that even though it was true they needed her property for the course expansion, they were also keen to get rid of her garden and, ultimately, remove the house that was associated with such a dark and tragic event— the kind that wasn't allowed to happen to residents of the Estates.

"And if he doesn't . . ." she continues, "well, I'm not too concerned about dying. Besides . . . whoever it was . . . they could've hurt or killed me if they wanted to."

"Don't you think if Ryan came home and you weren't there, he'd come over here?"

She nods. "He probably would. You're right. But I'd . . . I just want to see him the first moment possible. I'll stay over here some and check in a lot when I'm over there. How about that?"

"I wish you'd just stay here for a while first," he says. "I don't want to find Ryan and have to tell him that something happened to his mama."

"You just focus on finding him," she says. "I'll make sure I'm here when you do."

9

"Like on a field trip?" Kace is saying.

Not having her number or any other way of contacting her, Sawyer has just knocked on her front door and asked if she'd like to go to Psycho Suzi's with him and Rick Carson.

"Yeah," he says, his voice rich with sarcasm, "exactly like a grade school field trip to a crime scene."

They are standing on her front porch.

When she answered the door and saw him she had stepped out onto the porch instead of inviting him in. And, of course, she has the baby monitor in her hand.

"May not be a crime scene at all," she says. "It's not illegal for an adult to disappear of his own volition. And that's what a lot of people believe happen."

Sawyer shakes his head. "I know there are a lot of citizen cyber detectives who believe that, but . . . a lot of people believe the earth is flat too."

"So I take it you don't subscribe to that theory?" she says with a smile.

"Vanishing without a trace is nearly impossible," he says.

"Especially these days. Especially when so many people are searching for you. It takes a ton of money and a world-class new identity, and there's no evidence he had either. It takes precision and precise planning. It's not something you do impulsively after a night of heavy drinking."

"I don't necessarily disagree," she says, "but *nearly impossible* is not the same as *impossible* and it's a mistake to take anything off the table in an investigation like this."

"I don't disagree with that, but it's also a mistake to give every theory the same weight. I'm just saying that's one of the least likely scenarios. I think a big problem with unsolved cases like these is all the wild speculation and crazy conspiracy theories that take place mostly online. There's a false equivalency that happens in the many discussions. There's so much that's unknown and those gaps and voids and black holes get filled with outrageous and preposterous propositions based on no evidence. But because there's so little evidence, they don't get disproved either. I think if we have any chance of solving this thing and finding Ryan, we've got to focus on the evidence and what is most likely based on it."

"And I think we've got to examine every possibility," she says, "no matter how unlikely. If it was one of the most likely scenarios it'd already be solved."

She pauses a moment and he starts to say something, but she continues.

"The thing to do," she says, "I think . . . is . . . Why don't we put a little wager on it? One of us has to be right, right? Whoever is, whoever solves it first—or at least was proved right when it's solved—wins the bet. We just have to decide what, beside our pride, is at stake."

10

———————

*Y*ou *don't always have to act like such a bitch to him, do you?*

She is standing just beyond the left sidelight, watching him walk away through the sheer curtain, wondering why she feels the need to bust his balls so much.

Because you like him, silly.

I'm not in grade school.

Part of you still is. The part that finds herself liking a boy. *The part that acts like you don't like him, especially when you do. Playground Rules, bitches! Terrorize the one you're attracted to.*

But I love and adore Charles.

Of course you do. All the more reason to keep Sawyer at arm's length.

What is it about him? He's handsome or cute or whatever, has a nice, trim body, but that's not it. Those are pretty damn common even in Club Fat America. No, it's . . . something else. His . . . gentle, thoughtful, kind manner, maybe. His peaceful, confident demeanor.

Doesn't matter. All a moot point. Let it go.

I just find it curious. I'm not going to do anything about it. It's just attraction. Nothing wrong with examining it.

What purpose does it serve?

I don't know . . . Insight?

It's just a thinly veiled way to keep thinking about him.

I'm stopping now.

She returns to the small room where she is spending some of the best years of her life to find Charles sleeping peacefully.

Such a good, kind man.

A pang of guilt jabs at her, and she quickly sits down and takes back up the notebook and pen she had been working with when Sawyer's unexpected knock at the door made her set them aside.

She's working on an article for a caregiver magazine, finding catharsis in the process.

As you all are no doubt aware, a palliative care nurse is a nursing professional who provides additional and exceptional care for patients nearing the end of their lives. That's what I am, what I have been for the past few years. But that's not all I am. I'm also a wife and a homemaker. And all those things are far more related than you might imagine. You see, my palliative care patient is my husband, and the home I make is also the single-patient hospital I run.

And though my husband-patient has indeed recovered a few times, his illness ebbing and flowing, an ultimate recovery is not expected, not something I can even allow myself to hope for. I know too much. Have seen too much. My job as a nurse is to relieve patient and familial suffering by employing various and comprehensive appraisals of their spiritual, psychosocial, and physical needs, but I am also the one experiencing the familial suffering. I've often heard that palliative care nurses have to be the best of the best and the strongest of the strongest nurses, able to process the many negative and conflicting emotions with grace, strength, compassion, and resilience, but how much more challenging is that when the patient is or has been your world, was, in fact, the one who just a short while ago was taking care of you?

In addition to everything else, there is the enormous pressure I put on myself to give my dear, sweet husband the best care humanly possible. Think about it. I'm not just a loving wife who wants with all her being to ease his suffering and prolong his life with as much quality as I can, but I'm a trained, registered nursing professional. I'm supposed to be good at this. Check that—I'm supposed to be great. The wife in me holds the nurse in me to an impossibly high standard and judges me harshly when I fall short. And yet, the nurse in me does the same thing to the wife, just about different things.

I know I sound like I'm having a self-indulgent whine, but I'm trying desperately to do much more than that. I want to take all that I'm experiencing and feeling and surviving at the moment and turn it into something redemptive, to help others in similar circumstances. And I feel like just knowing I'm out here too will help. You're not alone. But, of course, I want to do so much more than just let you know you're not the only one going through the horror show you're going through.

11

"I can't tell you how much I appreciate you helping with Ryan's case," Sheri says.

It would be inappropriate for him to say he's looking forward to it or that it will be fun, so Sawyer just nods.

They are sitting on a wooden bench in her garden, surrounded by a thick, colorful tableau of rare flowers he can't begin to identify. Before Ryan vanished, this was a simple flower garden. Since then it had grown and expanded into a radiant and luxurious therapeutic garden.

There is a peaceful, calming, healing quality to this space, and he wishes he could conduct all his counseling sessions here.

"I'm glad we're meeting here today," he says. "This is such a serene environment."

"You can't imagine what I've been offered for it—well, for my home, mostly because of this, I think. It's obscene. But I could never sell. Not ever. I have to be here in case Ryan comes home. And the thing is . . . the Estates hates my garden and it violates all their rigid rules. The only reason they let me have it is because they feel sorry for me. The moment anyone else owned it, they'd make them take it down."

Sawyer looks around at the delicate petals of the vulnerable plants and thinks about the constant threat they're under from the elements, no less than the Estates.

"I still can't believe it's been two years without a single clue," she says. "How does someone vanish so completely like that—in this day and age?"

"Hopefully it's just that something has been missed, and discovering it will help unravel the whole thing."

"I have to tell you," she says, "I feel more hopeful now than I have in a very long time. I know you're . . . smart enough—no, that's not . . . you're insightful enough to . . ."

"Well, I don't know about that, but maybe just a fresh perspective," he says, "a . . . new set of eyes . . . will help. And not just mine, but Kace's too."

"She's such a dear," she says. "Deep down I mean."

He wants to ask her more about Kace, to comment in such a way that she'll reveal more about the intriguing and alluring woman, but he's made a commitment to remain single, to focus on grieving his relationship with Jules, to heal from it, and to be in a much better place before he ever even thinks about getting involved with anyone again.

"I just want to say," Sheri says, "if you don't have time to see me anymore . . . I mean since you'll be helping with the investigation . . . I absolutely understand. I'd much rather you work on finding my Ryan than shrinking my muddled mind."

"I should have plenty of time to do both," he says.

At his mother's request, he has been doing some light counseling for the residents of the Estates—mostly listening to them talking about aging and the challenges and issues it brings, even in a paradise like this. And though he gets the occasional client in a state of existential crisis, much of what he deals with is related to romance, relationships, and senior sexuality in a community where Viagra is as prolific as the rampant STDs.

But it has helped him—just having something to do, especially in those times when he feels he's been helpful to people in need.

He's been trying to fill as much of his time these days as he can, and though he knows he desperately needs down time to be still and quiet, to reflect, grieve, and heal, all his attempts at such have been counterproductive.

With even the smallest amount of time, he finds his mind spinning, careening out of control, pinballing off guardrails of guilt and regret, sadness and longing, and often winding up with him searching her social media to see what or who she's doing.

A former model, Jules was all about the physical and sexual, with little to no interest in anything related to the spiritual or psychological. Their connection had been primarily sexual, but he had made a project out of unlocking her hidden inner world.

She had told him that he was her last chance at romance, that if she couldn't make it work with him, she couldn't make it work with anyone. And though he believes that to be true, she also often said when referring to their friends who had broken up that the best way to get over someone was to get under someone else.

As closed as she had been during their relationship, he knew she would be infinitely more so now, socializing, popping pills, drinking herself to distraction, avoiding her inner life, suppressing her emotions, surrounding herself with the shallow and sick who are doing the same things, and probably sleeping with some of them.

The thought hurts his heart—all of it. Not just her being intimate with someone else so soon after what they had ended, but her sad, shut-off existence designed to keep her from feel-ing, which, of course, means she wouldn't only be anesthetized to the uncomfortable and painful feelings and experiences, but to the profound and joyful ones as well.

Are you talking about her or yourself? How can you sit here saying she's doing those things while justifying why you're doing them too?

You're right. I am talking about me. I've got to get back to . . . I need to get still, sit with my pain, process everything. Stop avoiding, distracting, rationalizing, justifying.

He has been doing some of the work of sitting with the pain and disappointment, letting go of the guilt and anger and frus-tration and recrimination, but not enough, not long enough and often enough. He's got to get back to his practice of medita-tion, contemplation, and the practice of letting go.

He decides to ramp up his journaling again and turn it into a blog. The regularly scheduled releases of a blog will give him the routine and accountability he needs.

And in this moment, the Breakup Blog is born.

He realizes Sheri is waiting for a response to something she said or asked. He has no idea what it is.

"I'm so sorry," he says. "Would you mind repeating that? I drifted off a moment."

"I hope to think about Ryan's case," she says.

He nods and smiles.

"Good," she says. "Like I said, take any time away from me to help find him. I was just wondering if he's still alive and how I'll handle it, whichever he is—or if I wind up not ever knowing."

"And what do you think?" he says, realizing he could've just said that instead of admitting he hadn't been listening.

"I don't know. Of course, I want to find him and him be alive and well, but . . . I also know the chances of that are . . . negligible at best. He wouldn't run off on his own. He wouldn't. And there's no way he wouldn't have come back when his dad died. Just no way. So . . . since there's not going to be a happy ending . . . I'll settle for just an ending."

Tears fill her eyes but don't crest. She blinks a few times and wipes at them.

"I understand," he says. "The not knowing has to be—"

"The part that drives me insane," she says. "Obviously, losing him is the worst and there's no comparison, but not knowing what happened to him or where he is or who took him from me is . . . slowly driving me mad. I mean it. It's no exaggeration. If it hadn't been for your mom . . . I'm not sure where I'd be. She's a special lady. It's no wonder you are the way you are."

He knows what she means, that he's a good counselor, a kind person, a gentle man, but almost laughs out loud because he feels like such a failure, such a fraud. How can someone who can't make a marriage work counsel anyone on anything?

His anger flares at Jules again. Why did she have to be so difficult, so closed, so emotionally stunted and relationally adverse? Her inability to let him love her, to love herself, had cost him far more than a marriage. It had upended his entire world. Making a relationship work with her had given him his platform, his brand, his messaging. Without her there would have been no book, no blog, no podcast, which would have been better than having and losing them because they now lack any credibility. It's laughable. She's turned him into a joke. Sure, the publisher should have never overreached with that guru bullshit, and he should have never gone along with it, but it wouldn't be an issue if she hadn't been utterly incapable of being in a relationship.

That's a gross overstatement and lacks the subtlety and nuance of what had really transpired, but he's angry and it's how he feels and what he wants to express—it's his truth in the passion of this moment.

He decides since his new blog will be anonymous, he can be as uncensored, real, and emotionally raw as he wants to be.

THE BREAKUP BLOG

I doubt this will help anyone but me, though I suspect many of you out there will identify with what I'm going through, relate to what I'm feeling.

Why don't relationships last? The vast majority don't. And though everyone knows that more marriages end in divorce than stay together, it's actually even more dire than that fact indicates. Far, far more marriages are unhappy than happy. And of those that don't end in divorce, how many devolve into an arrangement of cohabitation in a tense environment of strained civility?

Why, if relationships and marriages don't last, do we keep getting into them? Is it simply because some do and we keep hoping we'll get our turn at one that does?

Why are breakups so hard—even when you know it's what needs to happen? Why did it take me so long to actually do it? Why do I feel such a sickly sweet mixture of guilt, regret, relief, freedom, sadness, joy? Why do I feel like such a failure? Intellectually, I know that many, many relationships aren't meant to last a lifetime, yet emotionally, psychologically, I feel like anything less than forever is an epic fail. How can I feel so happy to be free, so confident it was the right thing to do, yet also feel sick down deep in the center of my core? How can it be that even though I don't want her, it bothers me that she so quickly got with someone else?

12

Psycho Suzi's occupies the front upstairs corner of a converted two-story old brick building on St. Bart's Bay. The ancient building had housed many businesses over the years, including a fish and oyster processing plant, and the lot it sits on is still surrounded by jagged mounds of oyster shells.

"He entered here," Rick Carson is saying as he opens the door next to Red Ralph's Raw Bar, "with Tad Roberts and Jennifer Oliver."

Kace has decided to join them, and the three of them step inside, Kace and Sawyer both looking up at the security camera above the door as they do.

The building is empty, the businesses closed. Suzi Lankford, the owner, has given Rick a key and unrestricted access to her establishment.

Pausing a moment, they look around.

A staircase next to the escalator, like the building itself, is rustic, weathered wood steps on an old metal frame.

A not particularly pleasant odor wafts over them and Kace

wonders how much of it is stale bar smell and how much of it is lingering oyster processing plant stench.

"They rode the escalator up to Suzi's," Rick says, "Ryan leading the way. He appears comfortable and relaxed and can be seen leaning against the balustrade as they reach the top."

Kace and Sawyer step onto the escalator behind Rick and the three of them ride to the top just as Ryan, Tad, and Jennifer had, Rick pointing out the security camera mounted on the ceiling and pointed toward them as they are slowly conveyed to the last place Ryan Shandling was ever seen alive.

When they reach the second level, they stop and look around.

To the right is a small alcove and the entrance to Psycho Suzi's. Straight ahead is another small alcove with what looks to be a service door. To the left is a mezzanine-looking area beyond which is a walkway that leads back to a movie theater and a few shops, which at the time of Ryan's disappearance was under construction.

"As they come off the escalator," Rick adds, "they disappear from sight of the camera. They go into the bar." He leads them the twenty steps or so over to the entrance of Psycho Suzi's and through the open doors.

Psycho Suzi's smells of stale cigarette smoke, spilled beer, the sweat from a thousand patrons, and the faintest hint of pee.

Directly in front of them is a square, dark wooden bar with black barstools lining each side, an enormous stained-glass wooden light box hanging over it. The bar is centered in the large space with tall tables spreading out from it on each side. Pool tables and dart machines fill a gaming area along the back right wall, to the left a simple rustic wooden stage and a dance floor sit idle, and both the men's and women's restrooms are along the back left wall, bearing the names *Psychos* and *Psychettes* respectively.

Beer logo advertising and memorabilia fill the faux brick

walls and hang from the black exposed-beam ceiling, and a huge black-and-white picture of Suzi looking her most psycho hangs high on the back wall of the stage.

"In here they drink more," Rick says. "By all accounts they had a ton to drink that night—and I can't help but think that's a factor in whatever happened to him."

"He would certainly be more vulnerable," Kace says. "More susceptible. Less capable."

"Less inhibited," Sawyer says. "He could've said or done something, intervened in something, and . . ."

"We know he and Tad got into an argument," Rick says, "but we don't know what it was about. Tad won't say and those who witnessed it couldn't hear the specifics."

"He's still top on my suspect list," Kace says.

"I agree he's not right and has actually been a hinderance to our investigation, but we have video footage of him leaving with Jennifer and never come back. And the time between when Ryan was last seen and Tad is seen leaving is a matter of a few minutes. I just don't see how he could've done anything, and if he did, how or where he could've hidden the body without it ever being found."

"Yeah, I haven't worked out how he could've done it," Kace says, "but I'm not ready to say he didn't."

"I'm not either," Rick says, "but I really can't see how he could have."

"How early in their time here did they argue?" Sawyer asks. "I'm assuming they split up after that."

"They did," Rick says. "Tad hung with Jennifer—mostly at the bar. Ryan went around talking to various girls, bought shots for different groups, listened to the band, and danced. It wasn't too long after they got here."

"Everyone who was here that night has to be a suspect," Kace says, "but those Ryan interacted with—and their jealous boyfriends or stalkers—have to take top priority."

"They have," Rick says, "but we haven't been able to track them all down. Lots of people paid cash so we don't even have their names. Certain small groups and individuals were unknown to staff and other patrons."

"What about releasing images from the video and asking them to come forward?" Kace says.

"I asked the sheriff about that early on in the investigation, but he may go for it now that nothing else has worked. I'll check with him again. Probably have to talk to him about putting you on the payroll too."

Kace laughs and notices that instead of Sawyer getting butt-hurt that Rick didn't include him, he actually nods vigorously.

"She's got a gift," Sawyer says. "My money is on her solving this thing."

"Be fine with me," Rick says. "I don't have to be the one to do it. I just want it solved."

"Y'all are sweet, but let's get back to what went down that night," she says. "What's next?"

13

———

"According to both Tad and Jennifer, even though Ryan and Tad had words and split up, they had all planned to leave together, so near the end of the night Ryan rejoins them. The last thing he says is he's going to talk to the band and will be right back."

She remembers reading how much Ryan loved music and playing guitar and how badly he wanted to be in a band someday.

"I can relate," Rick continues. "That's what I would've been doing. Ryan and I have that in common. I'd much rather be playing guitar in a band than investigating crime. Still don't know how I wound up doing this."

"How *did* you?" Kace asks.

"I truly don't know," he says. "I was . . . my plan had been to be a teacher—always loved reading and learning—and I thought it'd be a great schedule to also be in a band. Weekends off, holidays, summer break. Done every day by two-thirty. But . . . I was robbed. Came home to find my apartment ransacked, valuable stuff missing, graffiti spray-painted on the walls. Felt like such a . . . violation. And the investigator who came out was . . . so arrogant and ignorant and . . . couldn't've cared less about what had happened to me or how I felt about it. Told me he'd write a report, but nothing would come of it and not to get my hopes up about getting my stuff back. I went in to speak to his supervisor . . . and . . . and after talking for a while . . . he offered me a job and I took it—temporarily, I thought."

"Life is so . . . like that," Kace says. "Laughs at our plans, presents us with unexpected opportunities, never turns out like we think it will. Well, maybe it does for Your Love Guru dot com, but not for the rest of us."

Sawyer lets out a loud, harsh burst of humorless laughter.

The three of them are quiet a moment, each retreating into their own thoughts—presumably about the circuitous paths and capricious nature of life.

Eventually Rick says, "They never saw him again. They called his phone several times, but never got an answer. They waited out front for a while but eventually left, figuring he already had. They said he had done that before—especially here since it's so close to his mom's place where he was staying. And I should say . . . Tad and Jennifer's statements mostly agreed, but they were different enough not to have been coordinated. Really seems like they were telling the truth."

"That's good to know," Kace says.

"Who was the band?" Sawyer asks. "What did they have to say?"

"Hobo Girl," Rick says. "Four mid-twenties guys who say they only notice the girls who come up to them. Say that's why they play—for the women. 'Cept they didn't say it so politely as me. Say a few guys always come up and want to talk music or guitars and he may have been one of them, but . . . can't be sure."

"How soon after it happened did you interview them?" Sawyer asks.

"The Tuesday after the Saturday that it happened," he says. "Why?"

"It's suspicious that they are that vague about it—especially that close to it happening."

"Be worth going at them again for sure," Rick says.

Kace says, "Do we know for sure whether or not Ryan went into the restroom that night?"

Rick nods.

"With as much as he was drinking . . ." Sawyer says. "No way he didn't. Probably several times."

"We've got witnesses who saw him go in at least twice—I'm talking about when he and Tad came back later that night joined by Jennifer."

"Any from inside the restroom with him?" Sawyer asks.

"No, just going in."

Kace says, "How about coming out?" at the same time Sawyer says, "What about coming out?"

"Not really," Rick says.

"Can we go take a look at the bathroom?" Kace asks.

"Absolutely," he says, and leads them through the bar, snaking through the tables to the back.

The doors to the two restrooms are next to each other beneath a huge replica of the Bates Motel sign.

Inside the men's they find a huge all-white tile room with stalls on one wall, urinals on another, and a row of sinks with mirrors above them on another. There's a retro look and feel to everything that reminds Kace of the bathroom from the most famous shower scene ever filmed. And confirming that it's no accident that it does, every wall is dotted with faux round peepholes and the eye of Norman Bates looking through it.

High on the back wall is a rectangular window—the only one on the only exterior wall in the room. It's about two feet from the top of the ten-foot-high ceiling and measures about a foot by two feet.

"That's the only window," Rick says. "Only way out of here besides the door, but . . . it's too high to reach without help or something to stand on—and there's nothing in here like that. No chairs or ladders. Besides . . . even if he could get out it, he'd have nowhere to go. There's no balcony or ledges or anything, and even though we're only on the second floor, because the ceilings are so high in here it's more like the third or fourth floor. It'd be a forty-foot drop onto the concrete. Even if it didn't kill him, he'd've had broken bones and couldn't have walked."

"There's no way to make it to the water?" Kace asks.

Though the old building is on the bay, there's actually about twenty feet or so from the back wall to the water, where a concrete patio transitions to an asphalt alleyway leading to an old dock along the water where shrimp boats are sometimes moored.

Rick shakes his head. "Couldn't do it even if you have a running start and jumped with all your might."

"But what if he did go out the window?" Kace says. "If we're considering everything, we've got to consider that. What if he jumped and either was able to roll and not get hurt and walk away or got injured and somebody either helped him get away or killed him?"

"Except," Rick says, "the camera covering the back door and patio area would've captured him landing on the ground."

"Oh," she says, "right. Well . . ."

"What if instead of down he went up?" Sawyer asks. "Could he have accessed the roof and then come back in the building and exited some other way?"

"Theoretically . . . maybe . . ." Rick says. "But there again . . . all exits are covered by cameras . . . so even if he had . . . we'd've seen him when he exited."

"So that's what it keeps coming back to," Kace says. "His body has to still be inside this building."

"Not according to our exhaustive searches and the search and rescue dogs and later the cadaver dogs."

"So he didn't leave and he's not still in here," she says.

"See what I've been living with for two years?" he says. "It's enough to drive you mad."

14

───────

Sawyer says, "Are there any blind spots not covered by the cameras? Any first-floor windows? Any service doors? Where does the band load in and out?"

"Let's start with that last one first, then we'll look at the other doors and windows," Rick says.

He leads them out of the restroom, across the dance floor, and up onto the stage.

"If Tad and Jennifer are telling the truth," he says, "this is the last place Ryan was known to have been going, so—"

"Needs to be looked at more closely than anything else," Kace says.

"And we have, but yeah, seems most likely that whatever happened to him happened here."

"Are there any witnesses who say they saw him over here talking to the band?" Sawyer asks.

"One woman says she thinks she saw him near the stage at some point but can't be certain."

"If he came over when they say he did," Kace says, "the band would've been breaking down, right?"

"Right," Rick says. "They stopped playing around twenty 'til.

They have a simple set-up, use the house PA, so break down very fast."

"Is there any kind of green room backstage?" Sawyer asks.

"Two very small ones," he says.

He turns and leads them beneath the huge black-and-white picture of Psycho Suzi and through the plush black curtain into the dimly lit backstage.

About ten feet from the curtain are two small dressing rooms, no more than about ten by ten, and about five feet apart.

Kace looks down the corridor to the left. "What's down there?"

"A storage room and Suzi's office," Rick says. "And to the right, down this way, is the service elevator that leads down to where the band loads in and out and where deliveries are made."

"Can we ride down and take a look?" she asks.

"Sure."

They walk down the dimly lit hallway to the old freight elevator and ride it down to the first floor.

The service elevator is open and visible. If Ryan had been in it he would've been seen.

On the first floor it opens onto a loading dock large enough to accommodate beer and booze delivery trucks and band vans and trailers. The doorway outside, which is open, is a large commercial roll-up garage door.

Rick points up to the camera on the ceiling covering the elevator. "And there's another one on the exterior of the building that covers the area in front of the door."

"Can we watch the video footage you have from that night?" Kace asks.

He nods. "Sure. There's a lot of it. It'll take you a while to go through, but . . . you're welcome to it. Just don't post it online or anything. Probably lose my job if you do."

"Would never do anything like that," she says. "All I want to do is help figure out what happened and who's responsible. And if I do—or if I come up with any theories or anything—the only thing I'll do is turn it over to you. No one will ever know I was involved."

"Same here," Sawyer says. "How big was the band's equipment? Did they have flight cases or any boxes big enough to hide a body?"

"Maybe," he says. "See what you think when you watch the video. But here's the thing. If they took his body out in one of their cases, they would've had to then go back in with it a second time and get the equipment that was supposed to be in it the first time, and they don't do that. Still, we searched their cases when we interviewed them. We didn't do any forensics, but there was nothing obvious—no blood or anything—and they were all full of equipment."

Sawyer says, "I realize it's farfetched, but . . . since we have no idea what happened and haven't found him or his body in all this time . . . think we have to consider everything—no matter how outlandish."

"No, I get it," Rick says, "and I'm happy for y'all to do that. I hope you come up with something we've missed—or bring a different perspective to something we didn't that unlocks the whole thing."

"It's ridiculous to think we will," Sawyer says, "but—"

"Speak for yourself, Your Love Guru dot com," Kace says. "I plan on Sherlockin' the shit out of this thing."

"Well, I'll happily be your Watson," Sawyer says.

"While we're here, y'all want to step out and take a look at exterior doors and windows?" Rick asks.

Without waiting for a response, he walks out of the loading bay, beneath the rolling door, and out of the building. Sawyer and Kace follow.

"We've got this loading dock door," he says, turning and pointing to it. "It's got two cameras on the outside and one on the inside. Covers all of the loading area and most of the east side of the building."

Kace looks up at the cameras and then back down and around.

The loading dock is in the back corner on the southeast side of the building.

Across the side street is another old two-story brick mercantile building.

Rick follows her gaze. "That building isn't open to the public. Hasn't been restored or anything. Used mostly for storage, but it has external security cameras too. Their footage will be in what I give you, as well as other businesses, but all together they only cover a small part of the area. If Ryan got out of Suzi's somehow, which we don't think he did, there's a good chance they wouldn't capture him." He turns and starts walking north up the side street. "This is the only other door on this side."

A metal emergency exit door is set back in a small alcove, a light and a camera mounted on its ceiling.

"Two significant things about this exit at the time Ryan went missing," Rick says. "This part of the building was under construction and pretty dangerous to get through—maybe even impossible given how much Ryan had to drink. And . . . the camera here at the time was motion activated. It must have a slight delay because some of the footage we have only shows the door closing—not who opened it or if they walked through it. We think it was just when someone opened it and didn't actually leave through it—If they had it would've captured them, but . . ."

Kace is nodding as she studies the door. "Interesting."

"I read they poured concrete in there the week after Ryan went missing," Sawyer says. "Could his body be buried under it?"

"We searched it thoroughly and had both search and

cadaver dogs in there several times before we gave them clearance to continue working and pour the concrete." He looks up and points to the two windows near the top of the building on this side. "At the time Ryan disappeared, there was no second floor in this section, so there was no access to the windows on this side. And even if he could climb up to one of them somehow, why would he when he's already on the ground floor level with a door right here. Besides, no footage from any cameras—including the ones across the street—showed anyone coming out of those windows."

Kace and Sawyer look up at windows.

"We've already looked at the front," Rick says. "There's just the main entrance, which was visible by the security guards and the other patrons, so why don't we go to the back and then the other side."

They follow him back the way they came, past the loading dock to the rear of the building, beyond which is a small alleyway, a long wooden dock, and the bay, which at the moment is a little choppy.

Rick points up to two windows on the second floor near the roof. "That's the window of the bathroom you asked about," he says. "See, there's nowhere to go—no ledge to stand or walk on. Nothing. If he came out of that window, his only option was dropping or falling to the concrete below, which leaves him dead or severely injured."

"Could've then been dragged over and dropped into the bay," Sawyer says.

Kace nods. "That makes the most sense—that he somehow someway wound up in the bay."

"We searched the bay pretty damn thoroughly," Rick says. "And even if we had missed him somehow, his body would've floated up and been discovered or drifted to shore. But it's all pretty moot because the cameras back here didn't pick up anyone jumping or falling from that window."

"And no evidence of any kind was found out here?" Sawyer says. "No blood? No clothing? No DNA?"

"No, nothing."

"Was a thorough search done for those things, that type evidence?"

"We didn't run around taking DNA samples from random surfaces, but, yeah, we did a thorough search for any and all evidence—there just wasn't any. But like I keep saying, the video footage shows—"

"Video can be altered and edited," Sawyer says.

"Sure, but often not seamlessly enough so it doesn't show."

"How would you know?"

"Okay, sure. If it's so good we can't tell, we'd have no idea how many are missed, but I bet it's very, very few. But, hey, let me know if you see anything suspicious and I'll see if I can have someone at the FDLE lab look at it."

"FDLE?" Sawyer asks.

"Florida Department of Law Enforcement," he says. "Our state cops. They couldn't be the Florida Bureau of Investigation because FBI was taken. They assist small departments like ours—especially with forensics and lab work. They processed the crime scene. Their work is impeccable."

"But you raise an interesting point," Kace says. "Doctored video footage would make this impossible crime—or whatever it is—more explicable."

"I'm telling you the footage hasn't been doctored," Rick says, "but y'all see what you think. Just don't share it with anyone—not even experts. Especially not experts. Let me do that part so if this thing ever goes to trial we'll be righteous."

"Of course," Kace says. Then turning to Sawyer, adds, "That was a great thought. Might want to check to see if the domain is available for Your Investigation Guru dot com."

"Let's take a look at the west side of the building," Rick says, and begins walking that way.

Unlike the other sides, there are no upstairs windows on this side and only one small one on the ground floor—along with one door. Both toward the front of the building.

"So not only was this door and window covered by cameras here, but they could be seen from cameras on the building across the street."

Kace turns and looks at the antique nautical shop in the old metal building behind them.

"The other thing is . . ." Rick says, "this door and this window are in the restaurant and the staff was still cleaning and prepping at the time of Ryan's disappearance that night, so they would've seen him if he came through there."

"Every single possibility we consider," Kace says, "there's an ironclad reason why it can't have happened that way. Ryan came into the bar and never left the bar and yet isn't still inside the bar."

"It's truly an impossible crime," Rick says. "And yet there's no such thing."

"We're missing something," Sawyer says. "Have to be, but I have no idea what it is. There's no such thing as an impossible crime. No one can just vanish off the face of the earth."

"That's exactly what Ryan Shandling did," Rick says. "And after two years of examining every aspect of the case . . . it's enough to make me question everything—including shit as outlandish as the supernatural or alien abduction."

"You're joking, right?" Kace says.

"Sort of."

"Just making sure."

"I'm not a kook or anything, but . . . I'm tellin' you . . . a case like this . . . it gets to you . . . Makes you question yourself, question . . . everything. And not in a good way."

Sawyer nods. "I can imagine. Hope we can help some with that—at least share the frustrations and . . . I don't know . . . the burden of the insanity of it all."

"Most investigators never catch a case like this," Rick says. "I mean . . . work long enough and you're going to have unsolveds, but not un—I don't know—possible. I realize *unpossible* is not a word, but I think I need new language for this case."

Having seen all the possible exits, they follow Rick back around the building, through the loading dock, up the elevator, and into the backstage hallway.

"Only things left to see in the bar are the storage room and Suzi's office," Rick says as they make their way back down the dimly lit corridor.

15

———————

"The storage room doesn't have any external exits—no windows or anything. Suzi's has one window, but it's the same as the one in the restroom—no ledge or ladder or anything. Nothing to do but drop forty feet to the pavement."

He opens the storage room and steps back.

Sawyer motions for Kace to go first.

Such a gentleman.

They both peer in at what looks like a liquor store—shelves and shelves of booze in a room of about 13 x 20. Beer, wine, whiskey of all types and varieties. One shelf along the back wall is filled with all sorts of beer advertisements, glasses, paper products, straws, stirrers, and coasters.

She notices Sawyer carefully studying the walls and ceiling, and wonders again if Ryan could be inside one of the walls or up in an attic somewhere. *Can't be, though, right?* The stench of decay and decomposition would've been way too overwhelming to go unnoticed—even in a smelly college bar.

When Rick opens the door to Suzi's office they are

surprised to find Suzi inside, sitting at her huge black walnut desk.

"Sorry," Rick says, "didn't realize you were here."

"You're fine," she says. "Just came in a few minutes ago. Frickin' paperwork's never done. Bane of my existence. Y'all figured out where Ryan went yet?"

"Not yet," Rick says. "Working on it."

"I don't think we'll ever know," she says. "I really don't."

"Suzi, this is Kace Mason and Sawyer Payne," Rick says. "Kace, Sawyer, this is Suzi Lankford."

She's a fifty-something ex-stripper with longish bleach-blond hair made unnaturally thick by extensions. Her petite, narrow frame seems inadequate to support the enormous breast implants—the majority of which are showing through the deeply plunging white V-neck blouse that contrasts her dark spray tan. Her once pretty face is a network of fine lines, but it's the hardness of her countenance and wary, dark, shark-like eyes that most detract from her potential attractiveness.

The story on the street is that Suzi had been a stripper and then a house mom for the strippers of Jeff Holiday, a local businessman who has several illegitimate enterprises for every legitimate one, and that she only has her own bar because she blackmailed him for it. Kace has no idea if that's true or not, but more than one member of the community had told her that over the years.

"Kace and Sawyer are consulting on Ryan's case—unofficially," Rick says. "They each bring unique experiences and perspectives that I hope will help us figure this thing out."

"God, I sure hope so," she says. "Can't believe how long it's been and . . . just nothing. I won't say it hasn't been good for business. We get a lot of true crime types who come in to have a drink with Ryan, but . . . I'd gladly give up the extra income to get his poor family some closure."

Kace had read that Suzi had exploited her bar's connection to Ryan's disappearance in a variety of ways, including promoting it online and in social media, appearing on several true crime podcasts, and even naming a drink after Ryan—something she justifies by donating a small percentage of the proceeds to a GoFundMe campaign that supports efforts to find Ryan.

"Were you here that night?" Kace asks.

"I'm here every night," she says. "Businesses don't run themselves."

"You mind telling us what you remember?" Kace says.

"Did you see or talk to Ryan that night?" Sawyer says.

She nods, her dangling earrings tinkling as she does. "Yeah, I saw him. He was a tall, muscular, good-looking guy. Stood out, you know? And I knew him from before—used to come in every time he visited his mom. Usually with a girl, but sometimes without. He talked to several that night, but he didn't come in with one, wasn't hanging out with just one."

"How much was he drinking?" Kace asks. "How drunk was he?"

"He was pretty lit," she says. "Drunk people are my business. I can tell how drunk somebody is. And he was well into tying a good one on."

"So he was extremely vulnerable?" Sawyer says.

"Don't know about *extremely*," she says. "He's a big guy and he could still walk straight, but yeah . . . he wasn't at full . . . wits or capacity or whatever."

"Did you notice if he got into any altercations with anyone?" Sawyer asks.

She shakes her head. "They say he got into it with his friend Tad, but I didn't see it. He bumped into a few people, spilled a few drinks, hit on a few girls who were here with someone, but it was all just the usual stuff. Most of the people here by that point in the night were doing the same things. I'll tell you who you need to talk to is my bouncer from back then—Serge. He was paying much closer attention to everyone. I mean, if you're reinterviewing everyone. I know Rick has already spoken to all of us. Some of us several times."

Rick says, "I was thinking it'd be a good idea to let y'all talk to everyone you can without me sharing any of my thoughts or opinions or y'all reading my notes. Not color your thoughts or impressions in any way."

Kace nods. "I think that's a good idea."

"I agree," Sawyer says. "And it's possible some of the witnesses will be more forthcoming with a couple of amateurs than the police."

"I'm counting on that," Rick says. "Especially with a few of them."

16

———

When Sawyer arrives home, he finds his mother in tears and her small house in disarray.

"What's wrong?" he asks. "What happened?"

"I was trying to get Addie ready so I could go to my yoga class and she wouldn't cooperate."

He had seen some of Addie's tantrums and the way in which she could turn into a tiny terror when her strong will conflicted with the one attempting to be imposed on her.

"I . . . hate to even say it out loud, but . . . sometimes she's too much for me. I missed my class. I'm upset. The house is a mess. And she's still not dressed."

"I'm so sorry. I'll deal with her. Is there another class you can go to?"

She nods. "Have them all the time here—like everything else. It's like ice cream cones on a cruise ship."

"Well, take your time and don't worry about anything here, and by the time you get back we'll have the house picked up and a little attitude adjustment."

"Oh, thank you so much. What in the world am I going to do when you leave?"

. . .

HE FINDS Addie in her room playing with toys on her bed while watching Youtube videos about Disney princess toys on the TV on her dresser.

She protests when he finds the remote and pauses the video. "*Hey* . . . Turn it back on. Turn it on. Turn it on. Turn it on."

"I need to talk to you," he says.

"No, no, no. Want to watch princesses."

"Why didn't you get ready like a big girl for Nana?" he says.

"Don't want to."

"Sometimes we have to do things we don't want to do," he says.

She doesn't respond, just continues playing with her toys.

"Did you hear me?"

Again, she gives no response.

"Addie, I need you to stop playing with your toys and listen to me."

She gives the slightest shake of her head and continues playing.

"If you don't, you'll have to go in time-out," he says.

"No, *you* go in time-out, meanie head. You're being mean. I'm gonna tell my mommy."

"It's real important that you listen to Nana and me," he says. "We wouldn't tell you to do something that you didn't need to do. Okay? Now, stop playing with your toys right now or I'm going to put you in time-out."

She slings the toys and flops off the bed onto the floor and begins to cry and scream while writhing around.

He moves over to where she is and sits down beside her. "It's okay to be upset. Just let me know when you're better and ready to pick up your toys and talk."

She lets out a harsh little yell and kicks her feet.

"It's okay to be upset," he says again. "It's okay to yell and even kick, but it's not okay to yell or kick at me."

She yells and kicks again, but not at him.

"Take your time," he says. "Get all your upset out."

He pulls out his phone and starts swiping around social media, and before he's fully conscious of what he's doing, he's looking at Jules's posts, searching for insight into her life.

Though he knows better, though he's telling himself it's a mistake, he continues scrolling—ignoring himself not unlike he's ignoring Addie, who shows no signs of slowing down yet.

Relief washes over him when he sees that there are no posts with pictures of her with new guys—or worse, one new guy. As he continues navigating his way through her public expressions and declarations, he sees that there are no new pictures of her at all—not alone or with her friends.

He then turns his attention to the content of her posts, attempting to suss out her state of mind—how she's feeling, what she's thinking, doing. Next he looks at who has responded to what she has shared, searching for any signs that a new guy or even an old friend is suddenly responding with heart emojis and clever comebacks to everything she says and does. Spying a few new names and certain individuals who seem to be commenting on everything, he's about to click on them to thoughtlessly jump down the rabbit hole of searching for evidence on their pages, when, mercifully, Addie stops crying, sits up, and looks at him.

"You better now?" he asks, shutting down his phone and slipping it into his pocket.

She nods and sniffles.

"Come here," he says, and picks her up, pulls her into his lap, and hugs her. "Are you ready to pick up your toys in here and the living room and get dressed?"

"Will you help me?" she asks, her voice soft and raspy, coming out between sniffles.

"I will," he says. "And will you try your best to always do what Nana tells you?"

She nods.

The Breakup Blog

*W*HEN *I* WENT *through my first divorce, I said I'd never get married again. I was convinced that marriage was an oppressive and outdated form of contractual obligation motivated by fear, insecurity, and the desire to possess. And yet here I am. Not only with two marriages under my belt, but two divorces as well. WTF???? I was only ever going to have one marriage and I now have two divorces. I just can't. It's hard for me to even fathom. I look at myself as if I'm a stranger, a poor, sad SOB who can't make a marriage work. That's not who I am. It's not. Either of my marriages could've gone the distance and both of them had relatively lengthy runs—over thirty years combined. And I feel pretty good about both relationships. Each had a lot of good. A lot. And in both cases I popped the question because I knew it was what my partner wanted and needed. My mistake—at least part of it—was I didn't give as much thought as I should to what I wanted and needed, and what a long-term relationship with these particular people would be like.*

How can I have fallen into the role of savior and hero again? Why do I keep looking for someone to reduce? What does that say about me? Why do I pick partners who need so much? Why do I get off on giving them so much? Why must I be the white knight? Why do I need a project? Why do I get bored of them after a while?

My ex is a far better, more confident person and in a far better place than when we first got together. I'm happy and proud about that, but it provides me little comfort.

Some of us attach so completely, care so deeply, that even when we're the ones who effectively end the relationship and know it's time to move on, we find letting go so difficult.

Uncoupling is a process. It's not quick and it's not easy, and it may take years—sometimes long after the divorce is finalized, and maybe even after both parties are in new relationships.

17

Serge Birkin is a legit tough guy. Not particularly big, but big enough. Not overly musclebound, but every inch of him hard as a lighter knot. He's dressed in a tight but not too tight baby-blue T-shirt and dark designer blue jeans.

He owns and operates a titty bar called Pink Cheeks in a seedy part of the south side of town. Sawyer and Kace find him bartending, bouncing, and DJing during a slow shift in the middle of the afternoon, and though the joint is mostly empty, they sit at the far end of the bar by themselves for privacy.

Kace had said she didn't mind riding over here together, but insisted on driving. Sawyer didn't mind, and understood her need for autonomy and control, but found it surprising she didn't offer any explanation.

"I'll tell you this, guys," Serge says as he sets frosty glass mugs of draft beer in front of them. "I have not talked to anybody since making statement to the police. Wouldn't be talking to you now if Suz had not requested me to."

Rumor had it that Suzi had set Serge up with this place and had a significant stake in it.

Serge looks and sounds like Eastern Bloc, his accent and

speech patterns an English version of some People's Republic of Something a world away from North Florida.

"Well, we really appreciate you doing it," Kace says.

On the drive over, they had decided that they'd probably get far more and more valuable info if Kace took the lead and asked most of the questions.

"Give me moment," he says. "I will return."

He moves to the other end of the bar where three older men are seated, each with a stripper standing next to him, slowly nursing mixed drinks in lowball glasses.

Besides them, there are only three other people in the place —a stripper, the only black one here, dancing on the small, high stage in the middle of the room; a gaunt, ancient man on a high-back red leatherette lap dance sofa along the wall between the bar and the bathrooms; and the stripper sitting next to him.

Afternoons at Pink Cheeks are for older men who want extra attention and don't mind paying for it. There is no cover, half-price drinks, and the third-tier strippers who work it are not only nicer than the in-demand, pretty, young night-shift girls, but are more fully present, less distracted, and even more maternal.

"I'm gonna have to go back and forth," Serge says as he walks back up. "These guys are my most loyal and lucrative clients."

Sawyer is surprised to hear the word *lucrative* come out of Serge's mouth, but he shouldn't be. Just because the man looks like an Eastern Bloc mafia enforcer doesn't mean he's not intelligent with a decent vocabulary.

"No problem," Kace says.

"Excuse me a sec," he says.

As the song comes to an end, he steps over and lifts a mic from beneath the counter and says, "Give it up for Miss Destiny."

No one gives it up or even turns to look at Miss Destiny, who is wiping down the poll and starting to re-dress.

"Miss Destiny," he says again. "The beautiful and exotic Miss Destiny is now available for that special trip back to the VIP room for a little extra special attention. Coming to the stage now is Miss Martha Divine."

The stripper seated next to the ancient man on the lap dance sofa slowly gets up and makes her way through the maze of small, empty tables and chairs as Serge reaches under the bar and starts the next song, which not unsurprisingly is a country song by Ashely McBryde named "Martha Divine."

As Martha Divine takes the stage, Destiny takes her place over by the ancient man on the lap dance sofa.

Serge checks on the other patrons then rejoins Sawyer and Kace.

"You want to take your stripper name from a song, fine, but one about a cheating jezebel about to be killed by the daughter of the man she's schtooping . . . These girls, man. Am I right? Anyway . . . you want to know about the boy who disappeared. What can I tell you . . . Let's see . . . He was . . . He never sat down. Not once. Like a shark . . . always swimming."

Apparently, after revealing to us what appears to be his more authentic way of communicating he's going to stick with it.

"I'm not sayin' he didn't never stop," he continues. "He sees pretty girl, he stops, tries to chat her, you know, but he never sits, never stays in one place for very long."

"You think he was on something?" Kace asks.

"This, I do not know, but . . . my gut guess is yes . . . something. Not too . . . strong. I say . . . some form of speed, you know?"

Sawyer wonders if whatever he was on—if he was on anything at all—was from a week of staying up studying for exams or for powering through his exhaustion to party that night.

"And he was drinking too?" Kace asks.

"Like the watered-down drinks were actually water."

"How drunk was he?"

"Enough," he says. He then turns to Sawyer and says, "Hey. Man. Go tip the titty dancer on stage. Poor girl. Pair of tits like those and no one tips her. It's disgraceful. You go. Tip my girl while I talk to yours."

Sawyer glances at Kace, who gives him the slightest of nods.

"She will be fine, man," Serge says.

And even though he'll only be a few feet away, Sawyer realizes with a sinking, anxiety-inducing feeling that there isn't much he could do to stop Serge from doing whatever he wanted to—except try to reason with him or call the cops.

He stands and is about to ask Serge to break one of his twenties into singles as Serge places a stack of ones on the bar.

As Sawyer reaches for the stack, Serge brings his power hand down on top of Sawyer's and says, "Touch her tits, ass, or snatch and I kill you . . . I'm kidding man. It's joke. Serge is being funny man. Go have fun."

Sawyer pulls out his wallet and is about to pull out a twenty when Serge says, "Man, your money is no good here. Go have good fun titty time on Serge. But don't touch. Serge was not kidding about that."

Sawyer eases over to the four-foot-high stage and stands and watches as Martha Divine twirls around the pole, angling himself so he can still see Kace and Serge in his periphery. He had been hoping to be able to hear some of what they say, but the volume of the music is going to preclude that.

He's hoping that with him being over here Serge will speak more freely to Kace, but he doesn't like being this far away from her and not hearing what he has to say firsthand. He also feels awkward being over here tipping a stripper in front of Kace—even if it is with Serge's money.

"Hello handsome," Martha Divine says, her clear, classic Cinderella slipper stripper shoes clunking loudly on the stage.

"I bet you say that to all the guys," he says. "Even old Fred Flintstone over there." He gives a slight backwards nod in the general direction of the ancient man on the lap dance sofa.

She comes to the edge of the stage directly in front of him and squats down, her knees high and wide, the thinnest of G-strings covering her crotch, her bare, pear-like breasts undulating.

"Yeah, but I really mean it with you," she says with a wry smile.

He maintains eye contact with her as he has the entire time, and sees there's real wit and intelligence there.

She slides her finger down seductively and pulls open the strap of her T-back to let him place her tip beneath it.

Instead of sticking the money beneath her strap like he's supposed to, he hands it to her, his eyes never leaving hers.

"You really not going to look at my tits?" she asks.

"It's nothing against you," he says. "*Or them*. You're lovely and they are too."

"You're not gay," she says. "I can tell that. . . . You an ass man? I can turn around."

"I'm . . . I'm not here as a . . . ah, patron."

"You a cop?"

He shakes his head.

She glances over at Kace. "Oh, it's *her*, isn't it?"

"Not just," he says. "It's hard to explain."

"Try me," she says. "I'm smarter than your average bare . . . naked lady."

"Every Breath You Take" by The Police begins to play.

"She and I aren't together, so it's—"

"You're trying to impress her," she says. "Only have eyes for her tits, that sort of thing."

"Not exactly, no," he says. "I was just giving you the lay of the land. That was like background."

When he glances back at Kace again she seems uncomfortable and upset and is scanning the room with palpable paranoia, and he knows he needs to wrap this up and get her out of here.

"Gotcha."

"If she and I were together and we came in here as . . . customers, then we'd be up here together both tipping you and I wouldn't leer or anything but I wouldn't be opposed to looking. But since we're not together—in either sense of the word—and we're here working . . . I don't know . . . it just seems disrespectful—to *you* and her. It's dumb. I don't know. I just—"

"It's sweet. Truly. Kinda corny and whatever, but sort of sweet too."

She leans down and moves her mouth around his face and neck and to each ear, purring as she does.

"Hey," she whispers, "Corny Boy, whatever your business is with Serge, wrap it up and get you and your not-yet-girl out of here as fast as you can. He's a dangerous, brutal dude. He got this place by killing a man."

18

"You think she was talking about Ryan?" Kace asks.

They are in her car, driving back toward the Estates. Though not speeding, she is driving with purpose and intention, as if she is ready to be home.

Though still wired, she doesn't seem as upset as she did back in the bar.

What's that about? What's her home life like? Will he ever know?

"Just saying it's a possibility," Sawyer says. "Suzi blackmails Jeff Holiday to get her bar and Serge blackmails her to get his."

"Why would Serge killing Ryan give him leverage with Suzi?"

"He could've done it for her," he says. "Hell, she could've done it and he helped her bury the body. I know it's farfetched, but every theory is, and—"

"It's actually a lot better than most of the others," she says. "It would actually explain how he could have vanished so completely. Think about it . . . if it's an inside job. All they'd have to do is hide the body, close up, and go home like normal. Come back the next day or whenever and . . . turn off the cameras or put his body in something that nobody would question them carrying out."

"Or hidden him somewhere inside where he'd never be found—a wall or the foundation or something."

"It's the best theory so far in terms of explaining how he was never seen leaving and why he's never been found. But . . . the dogs didn't find him, so . . ."

"Wonder if he saw something he wasn't supposed to or . . . was having an affair with Suzi or if it was just an accident they covered up?"

She nods and says, "Doesn't explain why he or she or they would break into his mom's house in a Halloween mask pretending to be Ryan."

"True," he says, "but we have no explanation for that no matter who the killer was."

"If there *was* a killer," she says. "We don't know for sure there was. He could still be alive. That could've been *him* breaking into his mom's place."

"What else did Serge say?" he asks. "I thought he might tell you more with me gone, but if I had known he was . . . the type of person he is . . . I wouldn't have left. Not that I could've done much to protect you, but . . ."

"You did just right," she says. "He dealt that hand. We just played it. He didn't have much else to offer. He was mostly just hitting on me. He did give me the names of two guys who had words with Ryan that night, but . . . he could've just made that up to divert suspicion. He's never mentioned them before."

"I'm sorry you had to endure him hitting on you and—"

"It was no big deal," she says. "He wasn't crass or rude or anything. It was kind of sweet actually."

"*Sweet*?"

"I don't know. Doesn't matter. He's just that kind of guy."

"What kind is that?"

"Always on the make," she says. "Trying to sleep with virtually every woman he encounters. It's not about the woman. It's not even about sex. It's about the notch, the conquest."

"You seem to know a lot about him," he says. "Or about his type."

"Most men are pretty easy," she says.

"Oh yeah?"

"Most women too," she says. "Though not as straight-forward."

"So you've got everybody figured out?"

"Not even close," she says. "I said *most*, not nearly all. And just because someone fits in a particular primary type, doesn't mean that's the totality of who they are. Surely in your line of work you see that most people are pretty simple and some are extremely complex. I mean . . . honestly . . . how often do people surprise you?"

"Not often."

"And in your line of work they're telling you far more about themselves than most of us ever hear."

They reach the opulent, ostentatious entrance of the Estates and turn in.

Beneath planted palms, their fronds waving slightly in the wind, the pristine pavement shimmers in the sun as it snakes through the movie-set town with its quaint shops and mani-cured lawns.

"I can't get over this place," he says.

"How fake?" she asks.

"Most everything has an element of facade, but this place . . . It's all facade. It's creepy and Stepford."

"It wouldn't be if it were a subdivision or even a certain type of planned community," she says, "but the fact that they tried to make it look like an old town that had risen up organically and been here a while . . ."

"I can't believe my mom lives here."

"I can't believe *I* do," she says.

She slows down as most of the vehicles around them change from cars to golf carts.

"So what type am I?" he asks.

"Huh?" she asks, braking as a golf ball rolls across the street in front of them, followed by a sunbaked elderly couple pulling their large bags of clubs on rolling three-wheeled cart caddies.

"Man," he says. "Person. Human being."

"Oh. The complex type," she says. "You don't have a primary, simple, straightforward drive or motivation like Serge, but, hey, you tell me. You're the expert. No one's ever called me a guru about anything."

"I—that never gets old by the way," he says. "I think you're right. I think the same is true of you. And yet . . . nearly everyone is capable of the most stunning of surprises. And regardless, most humans are endlessly fascinating."

In their limited time together, this is the most personal they've been, and he can sense her pulling back, retreating to the semi-professional, restrained way she most often relates to him.

"Here's a question," she says. "Why would a man like Serge not charge us for our drinks and actually give you stripper tipping money?"

"Either he's trying to sleep with you," he says, "or he's trying to distract us from what a bad guy he is. Or both."

"I think your stripper is right," she says. "I think he's far more dangerous than he seems to be—and he seems to be pretty dangerous."

"She's not *my* stripper, but I agree."

"Did she give you her number?" she asks with a wry smile.

Martha Divine did in fact try to give him her number, saying he had treated her with more respect than any man she had met while working at Pink Cheeks.

"That's not the question," he says. "The question is—did I take it?"

THE BREAKUP BLOG

Is anyone out there? Anyone reading these? If you are, can you relate to what I'm feeling?

Why can I know you're toxic and not want you back and yet still care what you think and wonder what you're doing?

Why do I feel so guilty for being happy and doing well?

Why do I feel so hurt by how quickly and easily you seemed to move on?

Why do I repeat the same patterns and behaviors over and over?

Being married to her was a challenge. She was often very difficult, and she was never particularly warm or loving, and yet I find myself missing her, wanting some small part of the best of what we had.

We did have it good for a while. It was never without challenge, without difficulty, but early on there was some good mixed in with the bad. And some of it was very, very good.

I grieve what might have been, what we might have become—but truthfully, I was doing that long before we actually called time of death on our union.

I keep thinking about all the things she said to me—all the lies that weren't lies at the time, how she'd love me forever, how I was the only man she could ever love, ever be with, that if we didn't work out she'd never be with another man. She used to say that if I died she wanted to die too, that she didn't want to live without me. And she meant it. And I believed it.

Why if I don't want to go back can't I go on—move forward with the rest of my life? Or at least the next chapter.

Why does my interest in and attraction to another woman feel like unfaithfulness? I'm single. My marriage is over—legally and in every other way—and yet I feel guilty. How crazy is that?

I didn't want to get married again. I did it for her. She said she was scared I'd leave her, that being married would make her feel secure. So I bought a ring and proposed and actually married her and now I'm twice divorced. She wanted to be married but didn't want to do the work of making a marriage work.

Part of me is very proud of what I did—risking all for love, giving my marriage everything I had to give, making it work for as long as it did. Another part of me feels like such a fool, like an utter and compete failure—ashamed, embarrassed, depressed.

How to let go? How to release the pain and disappointment and anger? Feel it fully. Sit with it. Don't repress or suppress. Express it. Don't take it personally. Stop caring what other people think. Stop taking responsibility for anyone but yourself. Release the emotion, the pain, the hope, the expectation, the other. No one owes me anything. No one is responsible for me or my wellbeing. Release. Release it all—the emotions, the people, the attachments, particularly to outcome.

19

———————

She can't be certain, but Kace is pretty sure that Sawyer is behind the Breakup Blog.

So many things in it sound like him.

She wants to ask him, but figures nothing good can come of it. If it's him, it'll probably embarrass him and make things awkward between them. There's a reason he's doing it anonymously. If it's not him, he'll probably be offended that she thinks it is and things will be awkward between them.

But she doesn't have to ask him to know. She just knows. It's him.

It's so raw, uncensored, unfiltered. So vulnerable. No wonder he's not signing his name to it.

It provides real insight into how much he's hurting, what he's thinking, and how he's processing his anger, loss, and grief.

Through his pain, she can see a good man. A kind and caring healer who tries to do too much, who tries to save others, who takes on too much of the responsibly of the relationship and who is drawn to damsels in distress in need of love and care and saving.

She wonders if he'll ever be with someone who doesn't

need saving—or someone capable of saving him right back. She hopes so. He's capable of giving so much love. She'd like to see him be able to receive some too.

She finds his blog inspiring and wants to start one herself. And though she's started to write an article on being a nurse and a wife to the same patient, she doesn't see that being a blog. She needs something with more—

She's got it.

What if she did another expose? But this time instead of exposing the nursing drug addiction epidemic, she'll lift the lid on the vigorous sex lives of seniors living in retirement communities like the Estates.

There's so much to cover—the sheer number of sexual encounters and volume of partners, the game-changing impact of Viagra, and, of course, the astronomically high rates of STDs. A second sexual revolution is happening and it's largely unseen and unknown, and the seniors involved in it probably prefer it that way, but it's not going to be that way for very much longer.

Who's she kidding? Certainly not herself. Between taking care of Charles, running their household, and investigating what happened to Ryan, she has neither the time nor the mental and emotional bandwidth to investigate and write a piece like this.

It, too, can be another item to place on her *Hopefully I'll Get Around to it One Day* list.

For now, she'll keep reading Sawyer's blog and try not to envy him too much for his time and freedom.

20

Shanice Washington is a thickish, middle-aged black woman, surprisingly spry and agile for both her age and BMI.

She started helping her mother clean houses when she was twelve and never stopped—not even when her mom suffered a massive heart attack.

Over the years, she has built up a hugely successful business doing both residential and commercial cleaning, and has always been in high demand. These days she is the most popular overpaid maid in the Estates, but at the time of Ryan's disappearance she also had the contract for the janitorial services for Psycho Suzi's.

She cleans Sawyer's mom's place every other Monday while Robin takes Addie to the Estate's Grands and Grandkids playdate at the park. Unable to be in the house doing anything else, including work, while she cleans, Sawyer helps Shanice when she comes—particularly with the tasks he's most qualified for, lifting, scrubbing, vacuuming, and taking out the trash.

"You a sweet boy," she says. "Always helpin' me when you visit. All these years . . . You the only one who ever did it. Oh, a few times here and there somebody's mama might say, 'Grab that box for Miss Shanice,' but you the only one ever done it on your own. You's a sweet boy and you's a good man."

"It's not much," he says. "Wish I could do more."

"I'm sorry you're back here to be able to do it," she says. "You try not to show it, but I can tell . . . Bad enough bein' broke up, but havin' to move home . . ."

He nods and frowns. "And it's not even home."

"Ain't that the truth . . . all this . . . smoke and mirrors."

"You and Mom feel like home," he says. "And Addie does now, but . . . the rest of this place definitely does not."

"Well, you lick your wounds and do what you got to do and get up out of here, you hear me?"

"Yes, ma'am."

"Miss Shanice knows people," she says. "You're a good boy. Gentle and sweet. Easy to live with, easy to love. Don't you forget that. I ain't sayin' whatever happened with the young lady you's with was all her fault, but I betcha most of it was. You take your time this time and find a good girl, not one you have to do all the work for. You hear me?"

"Yes, ma'am."

"I know you a helper," she says. "Helps people with they problems. Helps me clean. But you don't need a wife who needs help. Find somebody who'll help you . . . take care of you. I wish my Wanda was a better girl . . . I'd fix y'all up faster than a chicken pouncin' on a june bug. But she's a mess. You don't need her kind of drama."

He smiles. "Be worth it just to have you as a mother-in-law."

"No mother-in-law be worth what that girl'd put you through. Promise you that. But that's what I mean. Nothin' is worth bein' tangled up with someone who gonna make you do all the work, who'll let you help her but won't help you back. Tell you what . . . you get interested in one . . . you bring her around and let Miss Shanice check her out."

"You bet," he says. "That's exactly what I'll do."

She nods to herself but doesn't say anything, and they stand there in silence for a long moment.

Finally, she says, "You seem like you got somethin' you want to talk to me about."

"Yes, ma'am, there is. I'm . . . trying to figure out what happened to Ryan Shandling."

She shakes her head and lets out a heavy sigh. "That poor boy."

"You had the cleaning contract for the bar at that time, didn't you?"

"For the whole building," she says. "Thought I wanted to . . . be a mogul, but . . . tryin' to get other people to work and do right . . . They ain't invented 'mount of money make that worth doing."

"Did you work anytime after Ryan disappeared?"

"The next mornin'," she says.

"See anything suspicious or—"

"A few things, but the biggest by far was the blood in the back hallway."

"Where?"

"Behind the stage," she says. "Where they bring in they instruments and stuff."

"How much was there? Where was it?"

"Mostly on the floor, but a little splattered up on the bottom part of the wall. Wasn't a terrible lot but it wasn't no little 'mount neither."

21

"I was never made aware of any blood," Rick Carson is saying. "And the crime scene team didn't process any."

"Are you sure?"

"Positive. Why didn't she report it?"

"She did," he says. "She told Suzi and says she's pretty sure that Jeff Holiday was there when she did. Suzi told her that she would report it to the police and for her not to clean it up."

"Did she now? 'Cause she never mentioned anything about it to us."

"Could she have said something to a deputy or a crime scene tech and you not know about it?"

"I don't think so," he says. "Because even if they had failed to tell me, it would be in their report, and in the case of forensics, they would've processed the area. I've read every note in the file several times. I've gone over and over all the evidence collected. This just isn't in there."

"Wonder why," Sawyer says.

"I'm gonna find out," Rick says, "but the most likely is that Suzi never reported it. It's unlikely anyone in our department or in FDLE wouldn't tell me as the lead investigator, put it in their notes, or have it processed."

"If Suzi didn't report it, then the question is why," Sawyer says. "And the most obvious answer is she had something to do with it."

"Or is covering up for whoever did," he says. "And who she'd do that for has to be a very, very small list."

"She strikes me as someone who only does things out of self-interest," Sawyer says. "I think it's far more likely that she's involved than she just did it to cover for someone else."

"I agree. Based on what the stripper said . . . it makes more sense that Serge is covering for Suzi than the other way around."

"And getting paid very well to do it."

Rick nods. "Yeah, neither of them strike me as the kind of people to do much of anything out of friendship or altruism."

"No doubt."

"This is great work," Rick says. "Y'all have already gotten info I never could. I'll follow up on this and see where it leads. What's next for y'all?"

"The band."

22

In the unreal utopia for active seniors that is The Estates, rec centers are all. The Bay Breeze Recreational Center is a huge bayside complex with indoor and outdoor components that include tennis courts, a huge swimming pool, billiards, bocce, darts, corn toss, shuffleboard, meeting rooms, picnic pavilions, dance, yoga, self-defense studios, a concert hall, and a music academy where Estates citizens can take lessons, perform, record, and pretend to be aging rock stars.

Sawyer passes by the fenced-in tennis courts where sixty- and seventy-somethings ease around the clay courts in the latest trendy tennis attire, volleying the small, bright green balls back and forth. He then moves through a tai chi class under one of the open air pavilions and around a belly dance class in the mirrored studio to the music academy in the back.

There he finds Terrick Bushnell, the former lead guitarist and singer for Hobo Girl, finishing a guitar lesson with an eager and enthusiastic gaunt, bronzed female septuagenarian.

After telling his student how awesome she is and fawning over her all the way to the door, Terrick turns his attention to Sawyer.

"Hey man," he says. "How's it going?"

As if just having come off the stage at a huge arena, Terrick looks like a rock star, all long hair, leather, tatts, earrings, bracelets, necklaces, big black boots, and a tiny, torn vintage T-shirt that hugs his narrow man-child torso.

"Good. Good."

"What can I do for you?"

"My mom is a resident here and I'd like to get her signed up for some lessons," Sawyer says.

"Sure, man, no problem."

"I can't believe she gets to take them from you," he says. "You're the lead singer for Hobo Girl, aren't you?"

"Was, yeah. We broke up."

"Ah man, sorry to hear that. I saw you guys a few times when I was here visiting my mom. Y'all were great—especially you. What a voice."

"Thanks, man," he says. "Much appreciated."

"And the way you play," Sawyer says. "You got sweet skills, dude. You really do."

Terrick brings the long, bony, tattooed fingers of his hands together in front of his heart and bows slightly in some sort of namaste-inspired expression of appreciation.

Sawyer says, "What . . . do they have Lebron James giving basketball clinics here too?"

Terrick places his hand over his heart and bows again.

"What happened to Hobo Girl?" Sawyer asks. "Who you playing with now?"

"One of those things, man. Still not sure what happened. Was good while it lasted, but . . . All good things . . . you know? We had a . . . One of the guys, Sebastian, our bassist, crashed and burned hard . . . and sort of took us down with him, I guess. It's still a mystery to me."

"You got your own band now?" Sawyer says. "I mean, I know Hobo Girl was like *your* band talent-wise."

"I'm working on a few things," he says. "Sitting in some with other groups when needed. Doin' some session work, and . . . teaching these lessons to pay the bills while I figure it out."

"Well, let me know when you get something going. I'll be the first in line."

"Sweet. Will do, bro. For sure."

"My mom babysits for my niece a lot," Sawyer says. "What's the best age to start with for lessons?"

"Depends on the kid, man, really does. Feel free to bring her by and I can evaluate her for you."

"Oh, wow, thanks. I really appreciate that. And we're happy to pay whatever your fee is."

"Evals are on the house for Hobo Girl fans."

"Thanks, man. I really appreciate that."

"Meantime let's get your mom signed up."

"Cool. What's the most lessons a week she can take?"

"Totally up to y'all."

"Is every day too often?"

"Not at all. I like it. Jump in with both feet, you know."

Bet you do like it, Sawyer thinks.

The former front man for the mediocre college band charges the outrageous fee of three hundred bucks for his VIP lessons.

"How soon can she start?" Sawyer asks.

"How about tomorrow?"

"Sounds good. What time do you have open?"

"Pretty much anytime she'd like."

"Cool. I'll get with her and get back with you, but I'm sure tomorrow will be great."

"Cool, man, just let me know."

"Will do." Sawyer turns to leave, but stops after a few steps and turns back around. "Hey, I have to ask . . . if you don't mind. I heard someone say you guys were playing at Psycho Suzi's the night that guy went missing. What's his name? Bryan something?"

"Ryan, yeah," he says. "No, man, I don't mind you asking."

"I just find that whole deal so . . ."

"I know. It's like a bad joke. Man walks into a bar . . . Never walks out again. Funny you mention it . . . That's when we started having trouble, man. Something happened to Sebastian that night. I don't know. He was never the same again."

"Sebastian? Oh, the guy you said played bass for you, right?"

"Yeah. Everyone called him Seabass. I don't know. He seemed like a pretty chill dude, but then he just changed. Never seen anything like it and I've partied with some strange cats in my time. He just cut himself off from everyone and started trying to drink and drug himself to death. Got no idea if he's even still alive. Doubt he is, given the way he was . . ." He shakes his head and grimaces.

"Someone said Bryan was going over to talk to you guys after your last set," Sawyer says.

"Ryan—"

"Oh, right. Sorry. Ryan."

"Yeah, that's what they said and he may have, but . . . I don't really remember. You always have some guys coming up wanting to talk about your guitars or sound or what not, but . . . I started playing the guitar to get girls, you know. Didn't really notice them if they didn't have tits."

"Is it safe for my mom to take lessons from you?" Sawyer says.

Terrick laughs, then answers as if it had been a serious concern. "Perfectly safe. I like 'em young, dumb, and tight—in both senses of the word."

There are far more than two senses of the word, but Sawyer assumes he means drunk and virginal, and he has a hard time keeping the disgust from his face.

"Any of the others remember Bry—Ryan? Anybody talk to him or anything?"

He shrugs. "Not really sure . . . Seems like Sammy said he talked to him, but he lies like a mother, so I don't know. This thing really didn't get big until we were already broke up."

"Anything happen out of the ordinary that night?"

He nods. "Was a weird night from start to finish. But really, what do you expect from a night like that. I really do think there's something to the veil between worlds being thinner on Halloween. It was all like black cat stuff, you know? Chaos unleashed on the world along with the tormented spirits."

23

Kace had always fancied herself a bit of a badass, and there were times as a nurse that she truly acted like one, but she has never felt like one more than today.

Playing the part of a badass rocker chick looking for a drummer for her band and maybe a lover for her bed, she is sexily and stylishly clad in a black leather cropped fringe jacket, black skinny ripped jeans, a slouchy gray tee, and a pair of black leather ankle boots with four inch heels that zip up the back.

Dropping a cigarette she didn't even pretend to smoke, she mashes it out on the sidewalk with the toe of her badass boot and enters Marvin's Music Store like it's lucky to have her do so.

Why do I wish Sawyer could see me? Why am I so tempted to text him a selfie?

The guilt she feels threatens to diminish her swagger, so she shoves it down for now and tries not to trip in her high heel ankle boots.

Marvin's Music is located in a large, old department store, its huge open space divided into sections beneath signs that identify them: Guitars—electrics hanging on most of one wall, acoustics in a temperature and humidity controlled room—Basses, Keys, Amps, Pro Audio, Drums, Accessories, Ukuleles, Sound Systems, etc.

Customers trying out new gear in each section create a cacophony of dissonant sounds that compete with instead of complement each other. Kace finds it jarring, and to her untrained ear it sounds more like showing off than test-driving new instruments.

She surreptitiously searches out Sammy Chastain, the former drummer for Hobo Girl—or is it the drummer for the former group Hobo Girl?—and promptly begins to ignore him.

Wandering around in a too-cool-for-school disinterested manner, Kace acts unimpressed with everything she sees as she makes her way to the back of the giant retail space to the bulletin board hanging on the wall next to the entrance to the restrooms.

As she does, she sees a couple of young employees start to approach her, only to be waved off each time by Sammy, who makes it clear in not very subtle ways that he's interested in far more than helping her find the gear she's looking for.

When he finally makes his approach, she is tacking up a notice for a drummer on the bulletin board.

"It's your lucky day," he says.

"Oh yeah?" she says, without looking at him, her voice thick with indifference. "How's that? 'M I the hundredth customer? I win a lame T-shirt or something?"

"I'm a great drummer and I'm in between bands at the moment."

She takes a step back and examines him in his cheap black slacks and yellow Marvin's Music sports shirt complete with name tag.

"Look like a gear geek retail drone to me."

"Don't let my disguise fool you," he says. "This is totally Clark Kent shit. I'm the best drummer around."

"What, around the store?" she says, looking around the store at the mostly young white males scattered throughout.

"No," he says. "In the region. Probably farther but I'm trying to be humble and not set expectations too high."

"You're doin' just fine there, believe me."

"I really am good," he says. "Believe me."

She nods vigorously. "Oh, okay. Sure. I'll just take your word for it."

"I can take you over to the drum section right now and impress the hell out to you."

"Good drummers are a dime a dozen," she says. "Doesn't take a lot of skill to bang around a bit, but . . . sane, sober, serious drummers are the unicorn of the live music scene."

"You're a sexy little ballbuster, aren't you? I love it. What kind of music does your band play?"

"The good kind," she says. "Any other lame-ass questions?"

"Yeah," he says. "Will you go out with me tonight?"

She shakes her head. "Not dressed like that, no."

"I won't be dressed like this," he says. "My buddy's band is playing at Psycho Suzi's and asked me to sit in on a few tunes."

"Exactly how bad do they suck?"

"Very little," he says.

"Suzi's is known for some lame-ass acts," she says.

"You can say that about every place 'cause most bands suck, but there've been some decent ones too."

"Last band that had the potential of being decent I saw there was Hobo Girl," she says, "but you could tell they were punk-ass kids and weren't about to work hard enough to live up to their potential."

"I was the drummer for Hobo Girl," he says, his voice rising an octave. "And I've been working my ass off since then. Do a lot of session and hired-gun work for major acts coming through the area."

"Oh yeah? Would I have heard of any of these *major* acts?"

"Probably not, unless you stay current on the up-and-coming artists of tomorrow."

"What does that even mean, *up-and-coming artists of tomorrow*? That maybe one day they might be a major bullshit pop disgrace?"

"Look, you looking for a drummer or not? Have a drink with me tonight and hear me play. Whatta you got to lose?"

"Hours of my short life I'll never get back," she says. "That's what."

24

As he keeps checking his phone, he wonders what percentage of his motivation is just wanting to hear from and interact with Kace and how much is wanting to find out what she learned from Hobo Girl's drummer.

He's on the kitchen floor with Addie, moving between various activities, including a tea party, a Play-doh pet grooming shop, Disney Princesses coloring books, and small action figures from a Nick Jr. show about a schoolgirl vampire whose family now lives among humans and operates a Scare BnB.

It looks as if the right front quadrant of Hurricane Addie made landfall here, but the chaos is limited to the kitchen because his mom and Sheri are hosting a game night for a few friends.

"Look at this," Addie says often about whatever she's doing at the moment, especially when he glances at his phone.

At this particular moment she's coloring the dress of a long blond-haired princess he doesn't recognize.

"That's awesome," he says. "Blue is one of my favorite colors."

"Mine too," she says. "It's too beautiful. Hey, color with me."

"What would you like for me to color?"

"Color this," she says, pointing to the long flowing locks stretched out behind the princess by the cold winter wind.

"Okay," he says. "What color?"

"Yellow, silly."

"Of course."

As they color and she hums various tunes he believes to be from the movie this character is in and makes occasional comments—some to him, others to herself—he thinks about how much he enjoys his time with her. They spend quite a bit of time together each day and he has come to look forward to it, finding himself in awe of her intelligence and wit, wondering how so much personality can fit in such a small package.

"Would you like a dress like this?" he asks.

She stops coloring in order to consider, lifting the crayon she's holding and tapping her lips with it in a grown-up manner far beyond her years. "Nah," she says finally. "It's not my style."

Unable to help himself, he laughs out loud in genuine joy.

Seeing his reaction, she repeats the line a few more times.

He realizes not for the first time that much of her extraordinary and grown-up gestures, actions, and phrases are the result of her uncanny ability to remember and mimic, and he wonders where she has seen or heard something similar.

"Addie, you're so funny," he says. "Such an amazing little girl. I love you so much and am so proud of you."

Though he makes a point to say these things to her every single day, she rarely responds, and on the few occasions she does, it's in her high-pitched cartoonish voice.

"Hey . . ." she says. "I have a great idea. Let's have a tea party."

"Let's do it," he says.

As she slides over to the little tea set he bought her earlier in the day during their shopping excursion for groceries and games Robin and Sheri could play with their friends, he stands and fills the tiny tea pot with water from the tap.

When he sits down across from her and places the tea pot with the small cups and saucers between them, she sort of lunges for him and wraps her little arms around his neck and says, "You're my best friend."

Tears fill his eyes as he hugs her tightly and he feels more warmth and joy than he has in far longer than he can remember.

"You're mine," he says, his voice hoarse with emotion. "I love you so much. You're such a special little girl."

"*Okay, okay,*" she says, her voice changing, taking on an *over-it* tone as she pulls away. "Let's have tea."

"You pour it for us," he says.

She does, her breathing changing as she leans over and concentrates on her task, attempting not to spill a single drop.

When she has poured both of their little cups with water from the pot, they each hold up their cups, pinkies out, and toast, each saying *bling* as their cups touch—something he had shown her once a few months ago and she had done since then no matter what they were eating or drinking. They have *blinged* plastic cups of Kool-Aid, powdered sugar donuts, Pop Tarts, juice boxes, pizza slices, and many, many other items.

Suddenly, there are four old ladies standing at the entrance of the kitchen smiling down at them.

"Oh, look, they're having a sweet little tea party," the smallest and oldest-looking of them says. Sawyer can't remember her name, but thinks it's something like Haddock or Hancock.

"Sit down," Addie demands. "I'll pour you some tea."

"Honey," Robin says, "if we get down there we won't be able to get back up."

"'Cause your skeletons are old?" Addie asks.

"Exactly."

In addition to her skeleton being old, Robin had spent some time on her hands and knees today, cleaning and weeding Philip Shandling's grave—something she does for her friend without her knowing it, something that would never get done if she didn't do it. Not that Sheri would ever know. She still holds such resentment against him for letting Ryan go out that night in the state he was in, she never goes to his grave.

Robin says, "Why don't you bring it in here to the dining table and let's have a tea party."

"*Yeah*," Addie says with her typical enthusiasm. "Let's do that. Come on, Sawyer."

"He'll be there in a minute," Robin says. "Miss Sheri and Miss Vivian need to talk to him first."

"You go on in there with Nana," Sawyer says. "I'll bring everything."

"Okay. I will."

He hops up and helps her up, then as she bounces over to her grandmother, he withdraws a cookie sheet from the cabinet, places the entire tea set on it, and follows them into the dining room area.

After he gets the three of them situated—his mom, Addie, and the small woman whose name he doesn't know—he rejoins Sheri and Vivian in the kitchen.

"Sawyer," Sheri says, "this is Vivian Waters. She's a dear friend of ours and has followed Ryan's case closely since he disappeared. I told her what you're doing and she wanted to tell you something."

"I told the police," Vivian says, "but I don't think they even looked into it. But of course they may have tried and been stymied by the Estates security goons."

Like his mom and Sheri, Vivian is living the good retirement life, the pale skin of her pampered face showing very little signs of her actual age. Her haircut and clothes are stylish and look like something a forty-something instead of a sixty- or seventy-something would wear. And like so many of the residents she is observant and knows far more about what's doing on around here than the Estates security give them credit for.

"My boy, Jackson, is handsome like you," she says. "He's also sweet and good with children. Such a good boy. He's also a gay."

Sheri says, "Gay, not *a* gay."

"Huh? Oh. Well, anyway. Not sure if that's relevant but I think it might be. Anyway . . . He was here visiting me and also went to that Suzi bar for the Halloween party the night Sheri's Ryan went missing. Such an odd phrase, *went missing*, isn't it? Anyway, he didn't think too much of it at the time, but he did later—after everything. He said an older man in a gay pirate costume with a big fake beard that covered most of his face was staring at him most of the night. Say he thinks he remembers him staring at Ryan and a few others too. He used the word *lasciviously*. He bought a lot of drinks for people that night—all men. My Jackson was one of them and he thinks Ryan was too, but says he can't be sure. Anyway . . . My Jackson was drugged that night. He can't be sure it was by the gay pirate guy but he believes it was. If one of his girlfriends—he has several of those, girls who call him their gay BFF—hadn't seen how out of it he was and got him home safely, I don't know what might have happened."

"Maybe the same thing that happened to my Ryan," Sheri says.

"When he got back to mine," Vivian continues, "he was so out of it. You could've done anything to him. We had to half carry him in. I called security and reported it, and they said Suzi's was out of their jurisdiction but they'd look into it and notify the police. When we didn't hear back from them, I called the police myself a few days later. They said they had never received a report, but that they would look into it and talk to Estates security and get a copy of my original report. Never heard back from any of them and got nowhere anytime I called either of them again."

"We just thought you should know," Sheri says. "In case it's relevant to what happened to my Ryan."

Sawyer wonders if when he's not around, his mom calls him *my* Sawyer.

"We will definitely look into it," he says. "That's very good to know. We'll also try to find out why nothing was done by the authorities."

"Who's *we*?" Vivian asks. "Do you have help?"

"No one's supposed to know," he says, "so don't say anything, but we're actually helping the lead investigator of the original case, Rick Carson."

"He seems like a nice young man," Vivian says. "Maybe you'll be the help he needs to finally solve the case."

"And that sweet child, Kace Mason, is helping him too," Sheri says. "Evidently she's been keeping up with and researching the case since it happened."

"The poor dear," Vivian says. "Don't see how she has time the way she takes care of her husband with no help at all."

Husband. The word feels like an unexpected blow to his solar plexus.

What does it matter? You're not available. You're off women, remember? Said you weren't gonna ask about her because it was moot. You knew a woman like her would be with someone.

"Think she has a little help now," Sheri says.

"Hospice?"

"Not sure. Don't think so."

Hospice? Is he sick? Explains her limited availability and that damn baby monitor.

"It's funny," he says, "I don't know much about her at all."

"She's very private," Vivian says.

"Guarded, I'd say," Sheri adds.

"She's so much younger than the rest of us," Vivian says. "Even before Charles got sick . . . she didn't really . . . mix with us much. And, of course, since he got sick we never see either of them. I offered to help her, tried to befriend her, but she wants nothing to do with it."

Sheri looks at Sawyer and says, "You're the expert, but I'd say there's some trauma there."

"Could be," he says, nodding slowly.

Probably is. What else have I missed?

"She's actually out interviewing someone right now," he says. "I should go check in with her."

25

———

"This is the place where that guy went missing," Kace says, looking around.

She and Sammy are seated at a high-top table not far from the dance floor, waiting for the band to start.

"We were playin' that night too," he says.

"Bullshit."

"We were," he says. "Was a weird night all the way around. Halloween party. A cluster from the start."

"Which one of y'all killed him?"

"Not me. That's all I can say for sure."

"Too bad," she says. "You could definitely be my drummer then. Nothin' more rock 'n' roll than murder."

He studies her for a long moment, seemingly trying to determine if she's serious. "Do I have to have killed a man or—"

"It's not a requirement or anything, but it'd guarantee your spot."

"What about helpin' a friend hide a body?" he says. "What's that get me?"

Her heart starts pounding as her entire being begins to tingle.

"More cred for sure," she says, "but . . ."

She tries to play it cool, but she feels anything but.

"What?"

"Anybody can say anything," she says. "Doesn't mean shit."

A young, skinny cocktail waitress with big fake boobs and no ass wearing black athletic shorts and a white Psycho Suzi's wife beater approaches them, order pad up, pen at the ready. "What can I getcha?"

The only thing more unflattering than the way the odd-shaped shorts fit her narrow frame are the supposed skin-color tights beneath them.

Sammy turns to Kace. "Get me drunk and I'll tell all—including where the bodies are buried."

She looks at the waitress. "I'll have a dark and stormy."

"Moscow mule for me," Sammy says. "Thanks."

Looking at Sammy for the first time, the waitress's eyes widen. "Hey, Sam the Man. You playin' tonight?"

"Just sittin' in on a song or two."

"Cool."

She hustles off.

Kace quietly takes in a deep breath and lets it out slowly, attempting to calm herself and slow down her thudding heart.

"So you didn't kill the Shandling guy, but you helped dispose of his body?" Kace says.

"That is not what I said."

"You did a good job," she says. "Two years and not even a whiff of him. You drum as good as you hide bodies, you're hired."

"I hide bodies as good as that . . ." he says, "I'm not about to tell you or anyone else where they are or that I had anything to do with it."

"So it's all just bullshit."

"Guess you'll have to figure that one out for yourself."

"Unless I get you drunk and loosen up those girly lips of yours."

"Girly?"

"Don't tell me no one's ever told you you have puffy, bee-stung, girly lips before?"

"People tell me they're big and sexy but not girly."

"Might want to start hanging out with some more honest people," she says. "Or not . . . If your feelings are as girly as your lips."

"What is wrong with me?" he says. "You're beating the absolute shit out of my balls and I'm lovin' every minute of it."

She nods. "Also fits with the girliness. Some loser beats the shit out of them and all they can do is clean up the mess and beg for more."

"Daaa-mn," he says. "I'd hate to meet the bastard who turned you into . . . this."

"Wasn't just one, I assure you."

She hops down off the tall chair, forgetting she has four inch heels on, and nearly goes down.

"You *leavin'*?" he says, the pitch of his voice rising and filling with disappointment and desperation.

"Simmer down, sweetheart," she says. "I just have to pee."

She makes her way over to the restroom without busting her ass, takes a moment to gather herself, splashes some water on her face, careful not to mess up her rock 'n' roll makeup, then returns to their table.

Though only gone for a few moments, by the time she gets back their drinks have arrived and the band is playing.

He raises the little copper cup his Moscow mule is in and says, "To badass rock 'n' roll bitches."

She points for him to put his drink down and he does. She then pushes hers over to him and takes his. "In case you slipped some date-rape shit in mine."

"If I did, that mean you're gonna date rape me now?"

Before she can respond or make an alternate toast, the song ends and he is called to the stage.

She sits down and begins to drink his drink as she listens to him play. She wouldn't know good drumming if it bit her in the tit, but the song sounds good and his playing neither stands out nor detracts from it, which she supposes is good.

He plays three songs, during which time she finishes off his drink, and by the time he reaches the table she feels so sleepy and out of it that she finds it hard to hold her head up.

26

S awyer texts Kace with a mixture of concern and disappointment.

He's starting to get worried. She should've checked in by now—actually, way before now. The music store has been closed for a few hours.

Is Sammy Chastain the killer? Does he have Kace?

As worried as he is, he's also sad and frustrated to find out she's married. He should've known and part of him even suspected it, but they had shared something, had a connection that to him was undeniable. It was for her too, right? Sure seemed to be. And yet . . . she's so guarded, so opaque, so very hard to get a reading on.

Doesn't matter. You're not supposed to be looking for a relationship anyway. Remember? Supposed to be healing and growing and figuring out why with all your education and study and practice and emphasis, you're a two-time loser at love.

He realizes the greatest sadness he feels isn't so much for the present, but for the hope she gave him for the future.

Let go—especially of the future. Come on. You know better. Let her go. Keep working on your shit. She's a distraction from that and you damn well know it.

I do know better. Come on. Get it together.

When she doesn't respond to his texts, he tries calling her again. When he gets her voicemail again, he leaves another message. "Please call me. I'm getting worried and just want to know you're okay. I'm sure you are and I'm being silly, but indulge my silliness and let me know, okay? Okay. Bye."

He disconnects the call feeling like an idiot.

And just then, as if she can somehow sense the state he's in, he gets a text from Jules.

I miss you.

He stares at it for a long moment, wondering how to respond.

She misses him. It's the first time she's said anything like that. She's never been a very emotive or expressive person, and when they had decided to divorce she had shut down completely—at least where he was concerned.

It feels so good to hear those three little words.

That she cares at all, let alone enough to miss him . . . buoys his heart up in the most warm and unexpected way.

How to respond?

He knows there's no hope of them ever getting back together, that he can never have with her what he really wants in a relationship, and his time away from her—a time when he has felt more like his authentic self, happy and free—has only served to confirm that, but he misses her too. Of course he does. How would he not? Should he just say that?

Miss you too.

He types the reply and sends it almost before he realizes what he's doing.

Can we talk?

Sure.

Now?

He checks his phone again for any word from Kace. Still none.

Sure.

When his phone rings a few seconds later, he steps through the laundry room and into the garage for some privacy.

"*Hey*," she says, her voice soft, sweet, tentative.

"Hey," he says. "How are you?"

"Not so good right now," she says.

"I'm so sorry to hear that, Jules. What's going on?"

"I just miss you," she says. "Feel so damn lonely tonight."

He can tell she has been drinking.

"I've been feeling a lot of that lately too," he says. "I know how painful it can be."

"Are we making a huge mistake?" she asks.

He wonders how much he should try to talk to her in her current state. He has no idea just how inebriated she is, but given the nature of her expression he guesses it's not an insignificant amount.

"It does *feel* like it sometimes, doesn't it?" he says. "We had so much potential and some really good times . . . especially early on, but—"

"Can you come over?" she asks.

"Well," he says, stalling, "I . . . I'm actually in the middle of—"

"Never mind," she says.

She's completely closed again, the windows of her soul shuttered, the door boarded and barricaded.

"I've got to go," she says. "Good talkin' to you. Take care."

"Wait," he says. "Please don't just—"

But she is gone.

Anger, frustration, and anxiety course through him, his concern for Kace's safety and his disappointment at discovering she is married, joining his agitation at his disastrous interaction with Jules.

He's got to do something with all this negative energy—burn it up somehow, use it for fuel for something productive.

He decides his time would be best spent trying to find Kace. But how?

He considers going to her house to see if her husband can track her location with his phone, but decides to make that his last desperate act if nothing else works.

He thinks about calling Rick Carson, but thinks that would be an alarmist overreaction at this early stage.

It then occurs to him to check Sammy Chastain's social media.

Bingo.

His most recent Facebook post says he's sitting in with a band at Psycho Suzi's tonight.

27

As Sawyer is pulling into the parking lot of Psycho Suzi's, he sees Sammy and Kace about to pull out.

At least he thinks it's Kace. It's hard to tell. Not only is she dressed like a rock star, but she's draped over Sammy like a—actually, she looks passed out.

As soon as he's in the parking lot, he finds a place to turn around, and when Sammy pulls his flashy red Kia Soul into traffic, Sawyer is right behind him.

What if he had shown up just a few moments later?

Yeah, but what if you had come sooner? he asks. *You could've kept her from getting into this situation.*

Whatever you do, don't lose him. No telling what fate awaits her if you don't intervene.

As he follows Sammy far too closely, he reaches into his pocket, pulls out his phone, and calls Rick Carson. It's his personal cell phone, and after several rings it goes to voicemail.

"I could be overreacting, but Sammy Chastain just left Psycho Suzi's. Kace is in the car with him and she looks unconscious. I'm following him now. We're headed east on 98. Call me back as soon as you can."

He wonders if he should just call the sheriff's department and report it, but decides to give Rick a few minutes to return his call first.

Traffic on the coastal highway is relatively slow and sparse. Sawyer is following far too close not to be seen, but he'd rather Chastain spot him than take a chance on losing him. It's not like this is some sort of surveillance operation. He's just trying to keep Kace alive. Rick can deal with arresting and making a case against Chastain.

Is Chastain the killer? Is that why he's doing this?

He feels a thrill of excitement at being able to finally find out what really happened to Ryan and where his body is.

Just stay calm. Saving Kace is all that matters right now. Everything else will come after you do that.

Chastain turns off 98 onto a desolate rural highway.

Sawyer follows.

The dark two-lane rural route is straight and flat and lined with acres and acres of planted slash pines—very few of which were damaged or destroyed by Hurricane Michael, the Cat 5 superstorm that decimated the region a while back. Somehow this swath of timber has escaped largely unscathed.

Sawyer phones Rick again and leaves another message updating him on where they are now.

As he's ending the call, he nearly slams into Chastain, who is turning onto a dirt road that runs diagonally back toward the southeast.

Sawyer keeps going straight on the highway after Chastain pulls onto the dirt road, but only for a short distance. As soon as Chastain's red running lights disappear into the woods, he stops, makes sure nothing is coming in either direction, then turns around and heads back toward the road.

Tapping 911 into his phone, he presses the speaker button and drops the phone onto the seat.

As he turns onto the dirt road, he tries to make out the numbers on the lopsided mailbox.

Just as the 911 operator comes on the line, Rick begins beeping in.

"911. Where is your emergency?"

"I had called Investigator Rick Carson first and when I couldn't get him I called you, but he's calling me back right now. I'm going to click over and take his call. And then he or I will call you back."

Without waiting for a response, he clicks over.

"I got your message," Rick says. "Where are you now?"

"A dirt driveway off 386. He just turned onto it and I'm following him."

"Okay. I'm on my way and I'll get deputies rolling. Wait for us if you can—unless her life is in imminent danger. We should be there in ten minutes or less."

Sawyer doesn't respond, and Rick is gone.

When Sawyer reaches the end of the driveway, he sees Chastain's car parked in front of a small rustic cabin, the driver's side door open.

Wishing he had a weapon or anything that might he use as one, Sawyer pulls behind Chastain's car and gets out, leaving his car running with the lights on.

Approaching the other vehicle, which is also running with its lights on, he sees that the driver's seat is empty. Walking a little farther, he sees that Kace is still inside, slumped over, seeming unconscious.

"Kace," he says. "Kace."

She doesn't respond.

He runs around to the passenger side and tries to open the door only to find it locked.

Rushing back to the driver's side, he presses the unlock button on the open door.

Running back around to the passenger side, he stumbles and trips over something on the ground and falls face first.

As he turns to get up, he sees it was Sammy Chastain who has tripped him and is now holding a handgun on him.

"Stay down," Sammy says.

His voice is high and tight with tension, his eyes are wide and crazed, and the revolver is shaking in his hand.

"Why are you following me?" Sammy says. "What do you want? Did you drug her?"

"She's a friend of mine. I was worried about her. Why is she passed out? What are you doing with her?"

"I don't know, man. I'm just . . . She's . . . tripping on something. I don't know what she took or if someone slipped her something. I don't know. But . . . wasn't me. I . . . I'm just trying to help her."

"By bringing her here?"

"I didn't know what else to do, man. I don't know her. She has no ID on her. Nothing."

"Why didn't you take her to the hospital?"

"I don't know. I just panicked. I didn't want them to think I had anything to do with this. I'm on probation."

"Can I get up?" Sawyer asks.

Chastain takes a few steps back. "Yeah, sure, but don't try anything. I'll shoot you if you try anything, and you're trespassing on my private property, so . . . you know . . . Stand Your Ground and all that."

"If you're telling the truth," Sawyer says, "I'm sure you won't mind if I check on her."

"That's fine. Just go slow. I'll be right behind you with the gun pointed at your head."

Sawyer lifts his hands as he turns around and slowly begins to make his way back around to Kace.

He's only taken a few steps when he hears sirens.

"You called the cops?" Sammy says.

"Yeah. Again, it shouldn't be a problem if you're innocent and telling the truth."

"Yeah, cause no innocent people ever got jammed up by the cops."

"Not many white ones," Sawyer says.

When the lights start flashing in the trees around them, Sammy takes off running into the woods.

Sawyer rushes over to the front passenger door, snatches it open, and pulls Kace up.

"Hey, are you okay?"

Her eyes roll back in her head and she mumbles something incoherently.

He gently slaps her face and shakes her a bit, raising his voice as he says her name again and asks her to wake up and stay with him.

A few moments later, he's surrounded by deputies with their guns drawn, yelling at him to slowly raise his hands and back way from the vehicle.

28

———

"He swears he didn't drug her and was just trying to help her," Rick says.

"Why'd he run?" Sawyer asks.

They are standing out in the hallway in front of the open door of Kace's hospital room. It is later that night. Sawyer has been here with Kace the entire time. Rick has just arrived after interviewing Sammy Chastain.

"You said he had a gun, right?"

"Yeah."

"Well, he didn't when we found him. Probably ran to get rid of it."

The small community hospital is quiet, its hard-surfaced hallways dim and empty. Both men are tired but also wired, especially Sawyer, his raw nerves just beneath the surface.

"I don't know," Sawyer says. "You really want to help someone, you ask for help there at the bar. You call an ambulance or you take her to the hospital. You don't take her to your secluded cabin."

"Yeah, it's sketchy. And yet . . . I'm inclined to believe him."

"Really?"

"He's begging us to give him a polygraph," Rick says. "And with his phone call, he didn't call an attorney. He called Suzi and asked her to show us the video footage from tonight that proves he didn't put anything into her drink. And I'm gonna tell you . . . it looks like he spent most of time playing drums with the band. Wasn't even with Kace much."

"So he may actually be telling the truth."

"Might just be," Rick says, "but either way . . . there's not a lot I can do. Unless we find video footage of him doing it or a witness comes forward . . ."

"Could you search his house and car for whatever drug she was given?" Sawyer asks.

"Not with what I have now. It's not like on TV. We actually have to have evidence to do anything."

Kace sits up in the bed, and they rush in to her.

"Where am I? What happened?"

"You're in the hospital," Sawyer says. "You're fine. Someone slipped you something at Suzi's."

"I've got to get home," she says. "Help me up."

Rick shakes his head. "You need to rest and—"

"I'll rest at home," she says. "I've got to get back there."

"I'm afraid you can't," Rick says. "You've been—"

"I'm afraid I can and I'm going to if I have to fall out of the bed and crawl."

"I'll take you," Sawyer says. "Here, let me help you up."

Sawyer steps over and extends his arm to her.

"She really needs to stay for observation and—"

"She cares for her husband," Sawyer says. "She has to be there."

Kace stops and looks at him. "Thank you."

"Okay," Rick says. "But at least let a nurse come and discharge you."

"They take way too long. I'm leaving now. Sorry to be such a bitch about it, but I've got to go. I need my clothes," she says.

Sawyer steps over to the wardrobe and grabs her clothes.

"And I wasn't drugged," she says.

"It affects your memory, but you were," Rick says. "Sammy Chastain says he didn't do it, but—"

"He didn't," she says. "I wasn't drugged. And he didn't drug me. Because *he* was the one who was drugged."

29

"I didn't drink my drink," Kace says. "I drank his. He drank mine and was fine."

"So somebody at Suzi's is drugging guys," Sawyer says. "Could be what happened to Ryan."

"I'm gonna go look at the surveillance footage," Rick says. "Especially around the bar. 'Cause it sounds like whatever was put in his drink happened before it ever reached the table. Hopefully Suzi will let me poke around behind the bar too. I'll be in touch. You get her home safely. Y'all get some rest and we'll regroup soon."

With that he rushes out of the room.

"I'm gonna need some help getting dressed if you don't mind," Kace says.

"Just tell me what to do."

"I'm just weak and sort of out of it."

"Of course," he says. "I won't look. Just tell me how I can help."

"Not really concerned about modesty at the moment," she says. "Just want to get out of here. I need to be home. If you could just get my panties and jeans started for me and slip my boots on, I should be able to finish."

"Sure."

He grabs her black silk panties and black skinny jeans and kneels on the ground in front of her.

She's sitting on the edge of the bed in her hospital gown, her feet on the floor.

Figuring it will be less invasive and more efficient, he decides to put the panties inside the jeans and slide both on at the same time.

She lifts her legs slightly, bringing her feet off the hard, cold hospital floor, and points her toes at an angle to help the process.

Though her gown covers everything above her knees and he keeps his head down and his eyes locked on the clothing in his hands, he can't but notice just how erotic this simple act is, how good she smells, how sexy her feet are.

He wonders if her toenails were already painted black or if she had done it to go with her rock 'n' roll persona.

Slipping her panties and jeans on, he pulls them up to about her knees, then pushes the rest of the jeans legs over her feet, bunching them up on her shins.

He can feel a stirring inside his own jeans, a rush of blood, and he tries to think of something unappealing and off-putting to stop it.

He finds her small socks and ankle boots, slips them on and then says, "What if I stand and turn around and you pull your-self up and steady yourself on my shoulders to finish?"

"You're sweet," she says. "So chivalrous to protect my privacy. Thank you. Let's try it."

"Feel free to put all your weight on me," he says. "Grab on if you feel like you're going to fall. And you can always just ease back into the bed."

He stands and turns quickly, hoping she won't notice the

new tightness in his jeans, and then backs toward her and bends down so she can grab his shoulders.

Instead of placing her hands on his shoulders like he had expected, she drapes herself over him, her head next to his, her mouth at his ear.

"Ready?" he asks.

"Give me just a minute."

"Take all the time you need," he says. "Just let me know when you're—"

"Okay, I'm ready," she says.

He wraps his hands around her wrists and very slowly begins to stand. "Is that—"

"I'm good," she says. "Weak, but not lightheaded or anything."

"Good."

Once they are fully upright, she removes her gown by releasing one hand and then the other, and he realizes she's nude from the knees up just inches away from him—closer in some spots. He can actually feel her breasts graze against his back as she moves about.

With one hand and then the other while holding on with its counterpart, she pulls up her panties and jeans and wiggles into her T-shirt and jacket.

"Okay," she says. "Think I'm ready."

Holding her right arm, he slowly turns around.

"Wow," he says. "You look amazing."

"I look a mess."

"Not at all. You look next level rock 'n' roll. A real badass."

"Thank you. You're sweet."

"You okay?" he asks. "Feel like taking those boots walking?"

"I think I do."

"Don't have anything else?" he says. "Purse or wallet or—"

"Nothing identifying," she says.

"That's what Sammy said—why he wasn't able to take you home."

"Didn't want to run the risk of having my cover blown," she says.

"How are you?" he asks, his eyes locking onto hers. "Are you okay?"

She nods. "I think I can walk with a little assistance."

"I don't mean physically," he says. "I would think this was all very traumatic for you."

"Really hasn't been so far," she says. "I've been pretty out of it for most of it. I'm sure later when I think about it . . . I'll freak."

"Well," he says, "if you need to talk . . ."

"Call Your Love Guru dot com?"

He laughs out loud along with her. "Exactly," he says. "Exactly. Anytime. Day or night."

30

"Was it him?" Sheri asks.

Her voice is quiet and flat like she doesn't expect it to be.

Sawyer has just entered the dark, quiet house to find her sitting at the dining table waiting for him.

He's a little surprised to find her here at his Mom's. Against his and his mom's and even Rick's strong objections, Sheri has continued to spend most nights at her own house, and he still can't tell if she's being brave, thinks the intruder might have been Ryan after all, or just has a death wish.

He shakes his head. "I don't think so. It looks like he may not even have done what happened tonight."

"Really?"

His weariness feels like it's at a molecular level. Completely depleted, all he wants to do is crawl into bed, but he steps over and takes a seat across the table from her.

"More likely he was the intended victim than the perpetrator."

"*Really*?" she says. "How in the world?"

He tells her.

"Oh wow," she says.

"With what Vivian said about Jackson earlier tonight," Sawyer says, "it makes me wonder if someone is drugging men at Suzi's and if it could be connected to what happened to Ryan."

"He was such a big, strong boy," she says. "I've always wondered how someone could've overpowered him. I've always thought maybe if he were drunk and there was more than one attacker, but . . . if . . . It would make far more sense if he were incapacitated."

WHEN SAWYER STUMBLES into his room, he finds Addie fast asleep in his bed.

He eases into bed beside her, attempting not to wake her, but when she opens her sleepy eyes slightly, says his name, and hugs him, he's glad he did.

He feels guilty for spending less time with her these days. She needs so much, this precious little being in the most formative years of her development.

He adores her, feels a real responsibility for her—one he's failing to meet in many ways right now.

Ryan's case is consuming his entire life. He's not spending enough time helping his mother, parenting Addie, processing his divorce, and dealing with his grief, and he's all but abandoned his Breakup Blog. And at this moment, he doesn't see any of that changing anytime soon.

31

She can't stop thinking about Sawyer. Not that she's really trying. It's a nice distraction from what almost happened to her tonight.

He was so sweet and gentle, so tender and gentlemanly.

His attraction, even arousal, was palpable, but he handled it so well, never let it get in the way of his care of her.

He was genuinely concerned about her. Who knows what might have happened if he hadn't shown up when he did. Maybe Sammy didn't drug her, but that doesn't mean he wasn't going to take advantage of the state she was in. Why else take her back to his place instead of staying at the bar or taking her to a hospital?

Unbidden, unwelcome, her thoughts turn to Cody and all the ways he had taken advantage of her. During their relationship, before she realized just how sick and twisted he really was, she had thought there were nights she simply drank too much and couldn't recall what they had gotten up to, but since then—in the minutes, hours, days, weeks, and years she's had to examine and process and perform a relationship autopsy on what happened—she's fairly certain he was drugging her.

She shudders thinking of what he did to her while she was unconscious.

Stop it. Don't go down that path. Think of Sawyer, of someone who is gentle and kind, a healer.

You don't know for certain that he is. It could be an act. Cody sure fooled you.

S*HE CAN'T HELP* but feel that Cody is closing in on her, watching her from the shadows of her life, waiting for the moment she is most vulnerable to pounce.

If that's true, why didn't he pounce tonight?

Maybe he was about to. Maybe if Sawyer hadn't done what he did, he would have. Maybe he's the one who drugged the drinks. His plan could've been to drug Sammy so he could snatch me.

He could be waiting for Charles to die.

That's probably what he's doing—enjoying watching me wearily work myself into an early old age and grave only to then come along to extract the last bit of life out of me in the most painful way possible.

Stop it. Get your mind on something else. This isn't the least bit helpful.

After checking on Charles, she returns to what she has come to think of as her Cat Woman cave and returns her attention to the surveillance footage from Psycho Suzi's and the surrounding businesses from the night Ryan vanished.

———

32

Ace Davis is a former Florida State football player who, thirty years after his collegiate career ended, still has big, broad shoulders, a trim waist, and a general muscular thickness everywhere, particularly in his arms, neck, chest, and hands.

He's wearing clothes tailored to accentuate his impressive build, including a green blazer with the Estates logo embroidered on the left breast pocket.

He walks with intention, as if he is always needed for something important, and perpetually has a radio wrapped in his huge right hand.

As the head of Estates security he wields a lot of power, but no matter how much it is, he carries himself like it's far more, like maybe he's top cop of the free world.

"Mr. Payne," he says, tossing his radio to his left hand and extending his right.

Sawyer shakes the man's huge hand and appreciates that he doesn't try to establish his dominance by crushing his smaller one.

They meet in front of the Estates security headquarters

building, which is located in the back of a building of quaint retail shops, which like everything else in the Estates looks both new and pristine and yet like it has been here for decades. A pipe and tobacco shop, a confectionery, an upscale toy store, a high-end toggery, and a golf shop all front the huge building with no other markings on it.

If Davis hadn't told Sawyer about it when he told him where to meet, he wouldn't have known what it was.

"I appreciate you meeting with me," Sawyer says.

"My pleasure," he says. "My job is not just to ensure our community is the safest in the world, but to reassure our residents and their families that it is by showing them how we do it."

Sawyer had asked to meet with the Estates head of security under the guise of questioning his mother's safety.

"If you'd like to come with me," Davis says, "I'll show you just how safe your loved one really is."

He leads him over to a John Deere Gator utility vehicle that has been repainted and branded with the Estates logos and badges.

"Hop in."

Davis drives like he walks, as if the fate of the world rests on him getting where he's going as fast as he can.

Sawyer buckles in and holds onto the handle mounted on the side as Davis races through the Harbor View town square with its huge faux lighthouse in the center, beneath the movie marquee touting both classics and the latest releases, around the many restaurants and shops, most of which are Estates-customized versions of national chains.

"Notice the street lamps," Davis says. "See how they're shaped."

Sawyer examines them. "Yeah?"

"Each and every one isn't just a light, but a camera. The same is true of traffic signals, signs, shop facades, certain trees

—especially around the golf courses. Most of those we added because of what happened to Ryan, even though it didn't happen here."

Leaving the square, he races toward the recreational center.

Slowing down a little in front of the huge sports and recreational complex, he says, "Look at that. See all the safe, active seniors?"

Sawyer looks at the wealthy, white, vibrant retirees playing tennis, pickle ball, shuffleboard, and corn toss, practicing Thai Chi, and taking dance, yoga, and exercise classes—all before the backdrop of the beautiful bay and beneath the benevolent sun shining down on them from a cloudless sky.

"Yeah?" Sawyer says.

"Not only are most of the instructors trained in security, but there are always Estates security personnel mixed in the crowd. They look like civilians, an adult son or daughter here visiting their parents—like you—but they're armed, highly trained security specialists. When we say this is the safest place on the planet, we mean it."

Sawyer nods and gives the middle-aged muscle man an *I'm impressed* expression, but inside he's troubled by the corporate big brother presence and surveillance state tactics on display yet unbeknownst to the tennis, shuffleboard, and pickle ball players.

Davis speeds off again, this time taking Sawyer to the front gate. Each Estate community has its own name, theme, architecture, and its own main entrance with a gatehouse and a guard.

"The real threat—not that there are any *real* threats to our security system—are from without," Davis says. "That's why we closely control who comes in. That means vetting the residents —though that's mostly done by the price tag."

Sawyer feels nauseous at the monied exclusivity implied in that statement.

"But it also means checking and double-checking everyone who comes in," he continues. "We don't have riffraff here—not as residents or guests."

"You mentioned that the enormous costs of living here prevents socioeconomic diversity, but I've noticed there's not a lot of racial diversity or—"

"We don't exclude anyone on the basis of race, religion, political affiliation, or sexual orientation," Davis says, "so if there's a . . . Well, let me put it this way—our communities are self-selecting. Some have more diversity than others, but we certainly don't do anything to create a quota, incentivize, or artificially inflate some sort of ridiculous ideal of diversity concocted by some ivory tower professor somewhere way up north."

Sawyer tries not to react, just nods and acts as if he doesn't disagree with Davis's bullshit rationalization for the wealthy white utopia they have constructed here along the Redneck Riviera where so many live well below the poverty line.

"We can lock this place down in seconds," he says. "No one in or out—and all from the command center."

Sawyer nods and acts impressed. "Could I see that?" he says. "You've showed me the cameras. Can I see the feeds?"

"I'm afraid civilians aren't allowed in there—for security reasons. You understand. Hell, most of my staff never get to go in there. Where are you parked? I'll drive you back to your car."

He whips the Gator around and heads back in the direction of the security building.

"What about Sheri Shandling's son, Ryan?" Sawyer says. "How did a member of this community vanish off the face of the earth like that?"

"Technically, he wasn't a member of this community," he says. "Just visiting. But even given that . . . it would've never happened if he had just remained within the safe confines of the Estates. I can't police and protect the whole world—would that I could—but I certainly can and do for everyone inside this citadel."

"But surely someone in your position with your experience and expertise has a theory about what happened to him."

He shakes his head. "I don't trade in theories and speculation, only facts, and unfortunately we don't know all the facts in that case. And probably never will. It's a sad business, but it's outside of my circle of responsibility, which is this amazing community right here. Just look at it. It's so beautiful and vibrant and safe."

"But what about the attack on Sheri?" Sawyer says. "That happened here. That's what has me so worried about my own mom."

"Our investigation is ongoing so I can't say much about it, but I will tell you this—you have nothing to worry about. Your mother is safe. It was an isolated incident and it's specific to Sheri and what happened to her son. It's become a very public case and there's a world full of crazies outside of the gates of this great place. But rest assured . . . the perp will be brought to justice. I'm seeing to that personally."

33

"Wonder if they can see us right now?" Rick asks.

"Probably," Sawyer says, and turns and waves toward the trees lining the golf course.

They are standing behind Kace's house waiting for her to let them in.

"It's so surreal that they have it," Rick says, "but then to boast about it like it's something to be proud of . . ."

"It was sickening."

"So much concentrated power," Rick says. "You know they never have turned over the costume Sheri's attacker wore. I'm telling you . . . they do what they want to . . . with impunity. Those who live here have far more to worry about from them than the supposed boogie men outside these walls they're meant to be protecting them from."

"No doubt," Sawyer says, "and—"

He stops as Kace opens the door. "Welcome to casa de Mason," she says. "Come into the war room."

She stands aside and they enter a Florida room that has been transformed into something resembling a homicide task force conference room.

"Well, hello, Clarice," Sawyer says. "This is amazing."

"I don't get out much," she says. "And I fancy myself a detective."

Rick turns to Sawyer. "What'd I tell you? If this thing gets solved, it'll be because of her." Turning to Kace, he says, "This is impressive."

"It's sad and kind of pathetic, but . . . gives me something to do."

"Don't do that," Sawyer says. "Don't be dismissive about this amazing work you've done. It's incredible—and how you're able to do it with everything else you have to deal with is astounding. It really is."

She blushes and looks away. "Well, thank you. I . . . Thank you. Bad habit. Downplay anything I'm especially proud of or feel particularly vulnerable about."

Sawyer is moved by her honesty and vulnerability.

"Well, you should be so proud of this and all the work you've done and are doing on the case," Sawyer says.

"He's right," Rick says. "I've worked with professional investigators with decades of experience that aren't as good as you two."

"Okay," she says. "Enough of all that. Let's talk about where we're at. How'd it go with Ace Davis?"

"Feel free to ask him yourself," Sawyer says. "He's listening in right now."

"What?"

He explains.

She shakes her head. "I've lived here for years and had no idea. Sure doesn't make me feel safer, though." *Except maybe from Cody.*

"Says if Ryan had just stayed inside the confines of this citadel he wouldn't've gone missing," Sawyer says.

"How does that jibe with what happened to Sheri right here inside her own bedroom inside her house inside this citadel?"

"Riffraff from outside must have snuck in somehow, but not to worry, top cop is on it."

"Always an outsider, isn't it?" she says.

"Stranger danger," Sawyer says.

"Exactly," she says. "It's what everyone wants to think. The danger is out there, not in here. Not in my family, my friend group, my community."

"Statistically, you're far, far more likely to be hurt or killed by someone you know," Rick says. "It's not even close. And yet . . . what happened to you last night . . . seems like the work of a stranger. We can find no evidence that Sammy did anything. Of course, I haven't found any evidence that anybody else did either."

"If Sammy's been going to Suzi's for years," Sawyer says, "why just drug him now?"

"That's a good point," Rick says.

Kace thinks she should tell them about Cody, but just can't. It's too embarrassing, too . . . She just can't.

"Maybe Sammy *wasn't* the intended target after all," Sawyer says. "Or maybe he's been drugged before."

"That's interesting," Rick says. "Both of those could be the case—or maybe Sammy was meant to be drugged so he'd be incapacitated when whoever did it made his move on Kace."

Kace shudders.

"Sorry," Rick says.

"No," she says, shaking her head and waving away his apology. "I've been thinking the same thing."

"Well, we can change the subject," he says. "Just know I'm still looking into it. Going over all the surveillance footage to see—"

"You mind if I take a look at it?" she asks. "See if I recognize anyone?"

"Not at all," he says. "That's a great idea—if you're up for it. I'll get the files to you."

"Surveillance footage was why I asked you guys over here tonight," she says. "I've been watching the feeds from the night Ryan vanished. Look at this."

She steps over to the desk with the computer and two large monitors on it and takes a seat.

Sawyer and Rick follow and stand behind her, watching as she begins moving the mouse around and clicking to bring up and enlarge video files.

"I still have a lot of footage to look at," she says, "but I wanted to go ahead and show you guys what I've found so far. Rick, you're probably aware of all this from watching it so many times, but . . . just in case . . ."

"I'd be willing to bet you've found stuff we've missed," he says.

"The first thing is this," she says. She clicks on a short clip of one of the external doors in which nothing happens. It's less than ten seconds and could be a still photograph, for all that takes place in it.

"What am I missing?" Rick says.

"Nothing," she says. "Nothing happens in it. Absolutely nothing. But . . . something had to trigger it. Some movement made the camera come on and start recording. I read something that said these cameras were notoriously slow to start capturing footage. What if the something that triggered it was Ryan leaving through this door, but he did so so quickly that he was gone and the door was already shut again before any footage was captured?"

"Interesting," Rick says.

"I mean, I know it could've just as easily have been a feather or a piece of trash blowing by, but . . . just trying to consider every possibility. And what if instead of just Ryan leaving . . . it was Serge Birkin leading or taking Ryan out? He might know that if he did it quick enough it would go unrecorded."

Sawyer says, "That really could be."

"The thing is . . ." she says, "it's the only shot like that. But I went back to look at other days of this same door—we have footage from the day before and two days after—and two different times it's the same exact footage except . . . in one of them you can just make out the door closing, which would seem to confirm that someone could've exited and the camera wasn't triggered quickly enough to capture it."

"Absolutely confirms it," Sawyer says. "Think about it . . . the camera is outside and is set to come on when the sensor detects motion. If someone were entering the building, it would be triggered by them walking up, putting the key in the lock, etc., but with someone exiting . . . it's going to be triggered when the door opens, but it only takes a fraction of a second to pass through a door, so it could completely miss the person leaving."

She loves the way his mind works and appreciates his support and enthusiasm for her discoveries—and does her best not to think about either.

"Two more things real quick," she says. "I know we all have somewhere we have to be."

She minimizes the file of the door and brings up footage from the loading dock and elevator feed.

"Look at this," she says, starting to play clips of the band loading out.

Hobo Girl can be seen carrying instruments and pushing large flight cases—two of which are large enough to hold a body.

"We had said if they put his body in one of these cases . . . they'd have to take it back in to get the piece of equipment that was supposed to be in it . . . but . . . look at this. They roll both these cases out, load all their equipment, and then a good bit of time passes—over an hour. It's very late. The bar has been closed for nearly two hours. The band is not drinking or anything. They've been loaded for a while, but they don't leave. Why? Then two strange things happen. First, this case is pushed out and loaded. Why so long after the others? But that's not even the most interesting part. I went back and watched the footage from them loading in. They only have two of these large rolling cases, and they have already loaded them like an hour before and then somehow they roll another one out. But it's not just another. I think it's the same case. Look."

She brings up two videos side by side on the large monitor. One shows the two cases being rolled out when all the other equipment was being loaded. The other shows the single case being rolled out by itself an hour later.

"See the one on the left," she says. "Look at the stickers. Look at the scuffs and paint and the way the band name is stenciled on it. I think it's the same case."

"You're right," Sawyer says, "it is."

"And check this out . . ." she says.

She pulls up another clip.

"While that case is being pushed out and loaded into the van in the back by the guitarist and singer Terrence Bushnell, Thompson Tait, the rhythm guitarist, is carrying this piece of equipment—which has no case or covering of any kind, and it certainly looks like it needs one—out the front door. But because he's exiting with the bartender and staff, it's easy to miss him and the fact that he's with the band. When they loaded in, he came in with everyone else. They may have all arrived in the van together. I don't know. But if they did, why didn't he leave the same way? Why would he walk out the front door carrying a piece of equipment, and where did he go?"

THE BREAKUP BLOG

I want to blame her for everything, of course, but obviously it wasn't all her fault. I'm to blame for a lot—like going in with the idea of changing her. I know better and yet I still did that. Still failed to just accept her just as she is.

I'm also to blame for not letting things go—for not forgiving her, for holding a grudge. If I had let things go more quickly we would've had a better relationship, a more peaceful household, a more productive time together, even if, ultimately, it wouldn't have lasted.

I was too critical of her. Sure I blame her for being so critical of me, so judgmental—even though I know it was because of how unhappy she is with herself. She's more critical of herself than anyone else. If she were more accepting of herself she would've been accepting of me, she'd be more accepting of everyone. And yet, I was critical of her too. I was far too quick to condemn, too quick to judge her—even for, ironically, being judgmental.

I'm guilty of not being more honest and direct with her once I saw our relationship wasn't going to work. I tried everything I knew to do to make it work, but I also wasn't honest with myself or her about the situation we were really in. She could sense it. She knew how I really felt, what I really thought, and she knew I was lying to myself and to a lesser extent to her that we could make it.

I'm to blame for having one foot out the door for a while. Not at first. Not for a long time, but toward what would be the end, once I allowed the futility to overtake me, I checked out. Stopped trying. Started looking for something else. And she could tell. She knew I wanted out, was halfway out, and yet I wouldn't pull the plug and pronounce time of death. She blames me for this, says I was trying to get her to do it, but if that's true at all, it's only partially true. The other truth is that I wasn't ready to give up—not completely. I was still holding on. Still holding out hope. I never consciously tried to get her to be the one to end it, but I can see why she would think that way. Ultimately, I gave her an ultimatum—make some serious changes or go our separate ways. If she was willing to go to counseling, to put in the work, I was committed and would be forever. But if she wasn't willing, if she never would be, then it was best that we called it quits.

34

The Copacabana Club is a '70s-themed bar and dance hall inside the Estates.

Lit with black lights and lava lamps, and decorated with psychedelic-patterned posters, disco balls, macrame owls, and Farrah Fawcett pin-up posters, the smallish club is filled with a purple haze of incense and tobacco and pot smoke.

Each dark retro round table surrounding the dance floor has an earth-tone fondu pot and a CB radio at its center, and four green, brown, and gold retro leather chairs around it. The CBs are how the patrons place their orders.

Beyond the tables, in the shadows along the back walls, a series of waterbeds serve as groovy seating.

The house band at the Copacabana Club, The Frayed Bell Bottoms, look like they're at a hippie-themed Halloween party or maybe a casting call for a live-action remake of Scooby-Doo. There are bell bottoms, of course, but also mini skirts, maxi dresses, tie-dyed everything, and plenty of headbands, scarves, chokers, and wood, stone, and beaded jewelry. All the guys in the band have huge hair, big bushy mustaches, and sideburns, and the female lead singer is sporting a Dorothy Hamill wedge.

When Sawyer, Kace, Sheri, and Robin walk in, the band is playing Marvin Gaye's "What's Going On."

Thompson Tait, the former rhythm guitarist for Hobo Girl, is now the bassist for The Frayed Bell Bottoms. Sawyer and Kace are here to try to talk to him. Robin and Sheri are here because when they heard Sawyer and Kace were going they said it sounded like fun and asked if they could tag along. And since both Sawyer and Kace thought it'd not only help with their cover but also their burgeoning attraction and sexual tension to have the older ladies with them, they said they'd be happy to have them come along.

As soon as "What's Going On" ends, the band goes right into Blondie's "Heart of Glass."

Seniors with various degrees of stiffness and immobility awkwardly move around the dance floor—at least half of them in some form of '70s attire.

As soon as they get Robin and Sheri situated at a table with drinks, Sawyer and Kace hit the dance floor.

Dressed in '70s attire, their plan is to make a splash with their enthusiasm for all things '70s, then approach the band on their break.

They dance to the end of Fleetwood Mac's "Go Your Own Way," then all of Michael Jackson's "Don't Stop 'Til You Get Enough," then have an awkward moment when "Let's Get It On" by Marvin Gaye comes on, but eventually ease into each other and find a comfortable position and pace to slow dance to the soulful, moving, and erotically charged song.

Her body feels so good pressed against his, and the scent of her hair sends him like nothing else has in recent memory.

They ease into a natural rhythm, their movements complimentary and comfortable. They are a minimum of two decades younger than anyone else on the floor, and it shows.

Wanting to break the sexual tension and intense intimacy

they're experiencing, Sawyer says, "It's like we're at our parents' class reunion."

"Yeah," she says. "Their *hundredth* one."

"I hope I'm doing as well and am as active when I'm their age," he says.

"You aren't now," she says, "so there's no way you will be then."

He laughs and the tension is broken.

"You know . . . we're talkin' to the members of Hobo Girl who are most accessible," Kace says, "and that's great. We need to. And they have been involved in some way, but . . ."

"The one who has exhibited the most post-crime change in behavior is the most likely to be the killer," Sawyer says. "From what Terrick said in his statement and from what I've read and seen online, Sebastian Lewinsky acts like someone who killed someone that night."

"Exactly. Just looking at the situation and how everyone has acted following it, I'd say if they had anything to do with it at all, Sebastian did it and the others helped him cover it up."

"I agree. We've got to find him. But we also need to know what his former bandmates have to say about him."

As the song ends and they stop dancing to clap for the band, the lead singer, a young woman named Kat, announces they'll be taking a short break, but not to go anywhere, they'll be back soon with more groovy tunes.

Before the band can get off the stage, Kace and Sawyer are there.

Handing her business card to Kat, Kace says, "I'm Kace Beattie and this is Sawyer Jennings. We own a string of clubs throughout the southeast and would like to talk to you about playing at them. I have no idea what a small place like this pays, but I'd be shocked if we couldn't quadruple it. Are y'all full-time? Do you play anywhere else? Do anything besides the '70s stuff?"

Sawyer is once again impressed with Kace's ability to inhabit a role so completely, to lie her ass off so convincingly, to embellish and react so adroitly.

"We're not full-time," Kat says.

"But we want to be," Thompson adds.

"We can make that happen," Sawyer said. "We've launched more than a few careers. We have enough clubs so you can play at a different place every night for three weeks—and they're close enough that you won't be in your van all day getting to the next one."

"We also do an '80s and '90s set," Kat says. "That's just because we play at two other theme clubs inside here."

"Y'all are very good," Kace says. "Nice and tight. With a really smooth vibe. You really should be playing for a hip audience that's not half dead. And y'all should know . . . our Nashville area clubs regularly have record producers in attendance. Do y'all have an agent or manager? Do you do any originals? Is a record deal something you'd be interested in?"

She just made that up on the spot, and Sawyer has to remind himself not to look impressed or surprised.

Thompson says, "Hell, yeah. I've got lots of original songs."

"You look familiar," Kace says. "I can't quite . . . put my finger on it, but . . . I feel like I've seen you somewhere."

"You've got her card," Sawyer says. "Let us know if you'd like to come in for an audition. I'm tellin' you . . . you get the gig and it'll change your lives."

"This is probably a long shot," Kace says, "but might as well mention it. We're in the process of producing a true crime TV series for Oxygen about crimes committed in or around bars and clubs. The budget is unbelievable. There's no money like TV money. So if y'all ever played in a place while a crime was being committed . . ."

As soon as the band had stopped playing, John Lennon's

"Imagine" had come up on the house system, and now Pink Floyd's "Comfortably Numb" is playing.

"I have the greatest true crime club case of all time," Thompson says.

"Oh, yeah?" Kace says, sounding dubious, skeptical, unimpressed.

"Yeah. "Ryan Shandling.""

Kace says, "That's where I know you from. You played with Hobo Girl. Good band, man. Didn't recognize you with all the extra hair and porn 'stache."

He nods and rubs his head.

"Y'all played the night Ryan vanished, right? That's one of the stories we're covering in our series. Suzi's given us full access. We planned to get one of the members of Hobo Girl to be in it. You got any juicy info . . . inside information or anything? If you do . . . Oxygen pays fifty-grand for a single interview—a buck fifty if they come back to you."

The rest of the band fades away, drifting off to take their break, as Thompson Tait edges to the front of the stage to stand directly in front of Kace and Sawyer.

Sawyer says to Kace, "If he has anything I bet we can get him three. Didn't Shandling say—wasn't one of the last things he said was he was going to talk to the band?"

"That's right," she says. "Wonder if they'd want the full band?"

"Why, when they could save a cool mil by just interviewing the one who will talk the most?"

"No, that's true. But they'd probably prefer to have the one who dropped off the grid . . . what's his name? Seabass."

"He won't talk to you," Thompson says. "But I will. And I can tell you everything he could."

Stevie Wonder's "Superstition" comes on, and the elderly men in leisure suits and the women in their disco outfits take to the floor.

"Whatcha got for us?" Kace says. "We get a finder's fee for you, but we won't go back to Oxygen without knowing what we have."

"How about this?" he says. "Sebastian Lewinsky killed the poor bastard and Terrick Bushnell and Sammy Chastain unknowingly helped him cover it up."

35

"Thompson, this is—" Kace says, attempting to introduce Rick to him.

"I know who he is," he says, his dismissive tone thick with derision.

Rick's presence may derail the entire thing, and Sawyer wishes they hadn't called him to join them.

It's much later, and Kace, Sawyer, Thompson, and Rick are standing behind the Copacabana. Robin and Sheri had wanted to wait for them, but Sawyer convinced them they needed to go home and relieve Addie's babysitter.

The dark night is turning cool following an early evening rain. A brisk, biting breeze blows through the trees lining the golf course across the way.

"He's a consultant on the show," Kace says. "Worked the original case. Has the best working knowledge of it. He was able to retire recently because of what we're paying him."

"Oh," Thompson says, his voice and attitude changing.

"We use him as a kind of human lie detector test," she says. "But he also follows up on any info that comes in. Attempts to verify it before it goes into the show."

"So tell the truth," Sawyer says.

"I will, man. Swear. Got no reason to lie. But . . . do we need to sign a contract or something?"

Kace pulls out her phone and tells Thompson to do the same.

"Record this with your phone too," she says, raising hers up in what looks like the selfie angle. "You recording? Step in here with me. This is a legally binding contract between Glamour Girl Productions and— What's your name again?"

"Thompson Tait."

"If Mr. Tait has truthful and useful information we can confirm, he's entitled to an on-camera spokesperson's commission of no less than thirty-thousand. Do you agree?"

Thompson nods. "I agree."

"Do you agree to tell the truth, the whole truth, and nothing but?" she asks.

"Yes, ma'am. I do."

How does she come up with this shit—and so quickly and smoothly? Sawyer thinks.

"Tell us what you got," she says.

"I ain't just gonna tell you everything for free," he says.

"Not asking you to," she says. "Just tell us enough to convince us you're worth paying a hundred Gs or more and putting in our show."

"Well, let me start by sayin' I didn't have anything to do with it," he says. "Didn't even know anything about it at the time. I ain't an accessory of whatever you call it—not even after the fact. I don't know for certain, so I'm not . . . I can't be arrested or jammed up in any way over any of this. These are things I put together later—after the events of that night, after learning that Ryan Shandling went missing. Okay?"

Kace nods. "Absolutely."

He looks at Rick.

Rick nods. "You can't be held responsible for something you

weren't involved in. From what I understand you sayin' . . . all you have is a theory anyway."

"Yeah," Kace says, in her bored and disappointed voice, "not sure that's worth paying for."

"Now wait just a minute," he says. "I have firsthand inside information."

She says, "Okay, well, let's hear it."

"It was such a weird night," he says. "Strange and eerie from Jump Street. And I know it was Halloween and the weather was all funky—most bizarre rain I've never seen—but it was more than that. Nothing went right. Everything was off. I realize that can't be one person's fault, but . . . it all began and ended with Seabass. Sebastian Lewinsky, our bassist. I don't know if he was on something or just having some sort of break-down, but he'd never acted like that before. Always been a pretty quiet and chill dude. Not that night. That night he was demon possessed or something. And think about this . . . we had been in a band together for four years, known each other for five or six, were friends—not close, but friends—had spent time together a minimum of three days a week for four years of weeks . . . and after that night none of us have ever seen him again. Ryan Shandling wasn't the only one who vanished that night."

"Not once?" Kace asks.

He shakes his head. "Not a single time. Tell me he didn't have something to do with it. And how about all that stuff about that night? Halloween and the rain . . . it's gonna make good TV, right? And I can describe it better, more . . . you know . . . fancy or picture it or poetry like or whatever. I can see it. Can't you see it?"

"We're gonna have to have more than pretty words and pictures," Kace says. "You got anything else or not?"

"Yeah. 'Course. I's just settin' the table. Now y'all come on in an' eat."

"Look," Kace says. "We got somewhere to be . . . so . . . get to it or let us go."

"Okay, okay," he says, "but just know I got all kinds of cool details and sub stories or whatever. There's a lot I can share. Anyway, the things is . . . that guy, Ryan, he came up to us when we finished playin'. Always have some that do. It's mostly women, thank Christ. Most nights we only went home alone 'cause we wanted to. But there'd be an occasional guy—usually wanted to talk about being in a band or guitars or tell us about some songs he had written. I remember this guy because he wanted to talk about all that stuff and he also wanted to help us tear down and load out, but he was pretty damn drunk. He was sort of a big guy—tall anyway, and could've been a help. We almost always used some of these talkie-talkie dudes as roadies, but he was so wasted—and that's sayin' something 'cause we all had been drinking a lot."

"Was he too wasted to help?" Sawyer asks.

"Let's put it this way . . . I didn't want him anywhere near my gear, but . . . he was one of those who insisted, you know? Wouldn't take *no* for an answer."

"Why didn't any of y'all tell me any of this back when it happened?" Rick asks.

He shrugs. "No offense, man, but it ain't our job to do your job. Plus, well . . . the others were more directly involved. I figured one of them would tell you. And, hey, you weren't offering three-hundred grand. No, seriously, I just . . . I don't know man. But I'm tryin' to do the right thing now. We both are, right? And we're both getting paid for it, so . . . win-win, right?"

"Keep going," Kace says. "He was wasted and wouldn't take *no* for an answer."

"That's right," he says. "I put my guitar in my case and got it out of there fast. He kept trying to help. I said, 'I got it. See if anybody else needs help.' He kept on. He knocked a few things over. Thankfully only like empty stands and shit, but still . . . And he just wouldn't go away. We were tryin' to talk to some girls, but he kept gettin' in the way and we had to keep grabbing our stuff before he could. Everybody was pissed at him and askin' him to leave but he wouldn't. Seabass said something to him—like piss off or something—and Ryan grabbed the girl Seabass was trying to talk to and kissed her long and deep, puttin' his hands all over as he did. And she started doin' the same thing to him. When Seabass tried to pull him off her, Ryan slung him back and he fell into his brand new bass and knocked it off its stand and it snapped the neck. It was brand new—a several thousands of dollars instrument—and it was ruined. Seabass threw it in its case and stormed backstage with it. Ryan followed like apologizing and shit and that's the last we ever saw of him. Disappeared behind the curtain and never came back out."

"That doesn't mean Sebastian Lewinsky killed him," Kace says.

"No, it doesn't, and I ain't accusing anybody of anything, but . . . if he didn't . . . why'd he do such weird shit with the equipment and—"

"What do you mean?" Kace asks.

"He comes back in a while later—without Ryan—and he grabs one of the large flight cases and rolls it back behind the stage. He's never so much as touched one of those before and now he's gonna load it—but he doesn't. Didn't know that until later, but he didn't load it. Later, when we have everything packed up—and he never came back in to help during that time—we start rolling our shit backstage and find him there. Not only has he not loaded the case, he's removed the equipment that was in it. He says he's takin' that equipment home to work on 'cause it's got a hum or a buzz or something—something none of the rest of us heard. Then get this— He says he's put some of his personal shit in the case and so put his own padlock on and please don't mess with it, he'll swap it out later. You may or may not think this sounds odd, but if you knew him you'd say this was the most bizarre thing he's ever done. All of it. Just nuts. He never worked on equipment. He never took any initiative. He never did shit. Then . . . if all that ain't nuts enough . . . he says he's going out the front. Now, he did have his own car that night, but . . . he parked in the back by the van. So what in the hell would make him go out the front just to have to walk all the way around? All this . . . taken with how he was never the same again and he's gone off the grid . . . I'd say he did it, but even if you don't think he killed him and put his body in the flight case—"

"What happened to the flight case ?" Rick asks.

"He came and got it later that night," he says. "Just took it off the van. Didn't ask. Didn't tell anyone. Didn't— The van was parked at Sammy Chastain's place. He's got a secluded cabin in the—"

"Oh, we know," Kace says.

"I think all of this is things your audience will be riveted by, but . . . just for the sake of argument let's say there's a reasonable explanation for everything he did . . . he'd still be the last person to have seen Ryan alive."

36

"Tell me we're not saying Ryan was killed over breaking a bass guitar," Kace says.

"People have been killed over a lot less," Sawyer says. "But I don't think that's what we're saying at all."

They are in Sawyer's car, driving back home from a long night at the Copacabana Club, looking as if it's 1977.

Before leaving, they had determined that Kace would examine the video footage again to see if any of it corroborates what Thompson Tait had said, Rick would try to track down Sebastian Lewinsky, and Sawyer would reinterview Terrick and Sammy to see if they can confirm any of Thompson's claims.

"You're right," she says. "It probably will come down to something trivial like that, but . . ."

"It's entirely possible that's just what started everything and something else happened in the back," Sawyer says. "Or maybe he didn't have anything to do with it. We won't know until we track them down and we may not even then."

"True."

"He could've witnessed something," Sawyer says. "He could be hiding out of fear."

"Or he could be dead," she says.

"He certainly could," he says. "Whatever the case . . . finding out should help us get that much closer to finding out what happened to Ryan."

"I know it's possible, but it's hard to see how they're not connected," she says.

"I'm happy to look at the footage for you," he says.

"Whatta you mean?"

"Or help in any other way I can. I don't see how you're able to do all that you do, and after what you went through at Suzi's with Sammy . . . You're so good at all this, but . . . it seems like it's all way too much with everything else you have on you, and . . . I just . . . Please just let me help with anything I can."

"Thank you," she says. "That's so sweet, but . . . honestly . . . working this case is the most fun and fulfilling thing I've done in years. Right now . . . it's what I look forward to the most. I actually feel guilty sometimes for how much I'm enjoying it— both because of the time away from Charles and because of the underlying tragedy it represents for Ryan and Sheri, but . . ."

"Well, maybe I can help with some of the other things you have on you," he says. "Household chores or repairs, caring for Charles, anything like that you need . . . I'd be happy to. It'd be a way of contributing to the case because freeing you up to work on it is our best chance of solving this thing."

She has to blink back tears and swallow before responding. "Thank you so much . . . You . . . You can't know what that means. And . . . don't be surprised if I take you up on it."

"I'll be very disappointed if you don't."

When they arrive back in their neighborhood, Sawyer pulls over in front of Kace's place and hops out. By the time he makes it around the vehicle, she has already opened her own door, but he can still walk her up to her house and see her in safely.

"You really don't have to—"

"Yes, I do," he says. "It only takes a moment and it's—"

Seemingly out of nowhere, Serge Birkin steps in front of them.

"See?" he says. "Chivalry is not dead, is it? Not in this pretend place, not when Mr. Payne is around, no?"

Sawyer takes a quick look around. Serge is alone, and though he no doubt has a weapon on him—likely more than one—none are visible. And yet his presence and his seemingly innocuous words carry a palpable menace, an undeniable threat.

He wonders if the Estates security surveillance monitoring team is watching them right now. Even if they are, can they tell Serge is threatening them or does it just look like three people having a normal conversation?

"Look at you two," he says. "Hippie dress, no? And yet Halloween is not yet I think. This how do you say . . . dry run? Pre-game?"

Neither of them respond.

"Payne," he says. "Interesting name. I wonder, man, how much pain you two have experienced. I do not mean what passes for pain in the first world. I mean true, existential pain, the kind that makes a man happily betray all that he considers holy. I know, I know, it is hard to imagine such pain in a place like this, but I assure you, it is possible everywhere, even a place like this."

Kace's hand had already been in her purse searching for her keys when he had stepped out of the darkness in front of them, and now Sawyer thinks she's slowly and quietly searching the '70s-era macrame handbag for the mace she told him she never leaves home without.

Does Serge notice what she's doing? Does he care?

"Just . . . ah, hypothetical . . . How much pain do you think you could endure before begging me to hurt her instead? It is interesting question, is it not? Here is another . . . Do you think you could stop me from hurting her, Mr. Walk-Her-to-Her-

Door-Chivalry?"

"I'd rather not have to find out," Sawyer says.

"That is very smart," Serge says. "I like this answer. It is good for a man to know what he is. You, for instance, are no tough guy, are you?"

Sawyer shakes his head.

"See? That is good to know, my friend. And yet . . . both of you . . . in your hippie Halloween dress . . . are attempting to do tough-guy things. You see the problem, my man? You say you are not tough guy—and you are right—and yet you are attempting to do tough-guy activities. It is very confusing. So it is simple. You don't want to find out any answers to Serge's questions. You do not want to know how much pain you can endure before begging me to hurt her instead. You do not want to see if you could even slow me down a little from hurting her. The solution is so obvious. I'm sure you have reached this conclusion already. Stop with these activities—both of you— and you never see Serge again, never have to answer Serge's existential questions."

They both nod, but don't say anything.

"This lead to opposite flip coin side," he says. "If you do not stop this what you are doing . . . you get Serge existential pain test."

Without another word he is gone, vanishing in the dark night like a bad dream leaving wisps of terror in its wake.

Sawyer turns to Kace. "Are you okay?"

"No."

"I'm so sorry about that," he says.

"Why are you—"

"That I couldn't . . . that I wouldn't have been able to protect you from . . . I would've tried, and maybe you could have run away while we were . . . but I've never felt so weak and power- less in my entire life."

"To match a man like that you'd have to be a man like that," she says. "Don't apologize for not being a sadistic sociopath."

"Let's get you inside," he says. "I'm gonna call Rick and let him know. Maybe he can put a deputy on your house tonight."

"And the next night and the next?" she says. "As much as I don't want to . . . we've got to stop. It's not just us who would get hurt. Think about your mom and Sheri and Addie. And I've got to think about Charles. I don't want to stop, but . . . I mean, I *really* don't want to. We're getting somewhere."

Sawyer nods. "He wouldn't have felt the need to threaten us if we weren't."

"Exactly," she says. "But who was he threatening us for—just himself? Suzi? Sebastian and the band? He didn't come threaten us after we spoke to him or Suzi—only after we spoke to Thompson and the other band members."

"One of them could've tipped off Sebastian and he sent Serge. Just no way to know. And I guess now we never will—unless Rick can close it. Maybe we've given him enough so he can. "But I worry about him too. I don't think someone like Serge is just a threat to civilians."

"So we're sayin' we're gonna quit and warn Rick," she says.

"I think we have to," he says. "I wish we didn't, but . . . I don't want to put you in any more danger. Don't want to risk Mom or Addie or anyone else getting hurt."

She says, "Do you think it's possible it was Serge who broke into Sheri's house the other night?"

"I think she would've mentioned his accent."

"I meant could he have been behind it."

"Could be," he says. "He could be behind all of it—or at least the one doing the dirty work for whoever's really behind it. But I still don't understand the purpose of the break-in. Can't see how it fits with . . . 'Course I can't see how any of this fits together."

"And now we never will," she says.

37

"Oh my God," Sheri says. "Well, y'all have to stop immediately. No way I'm taking a chance on Robin going through what I went through. I'd die before I'd let a friend lose a child."

She and Robin had been waiting for him, anxious to find out what he had learned from Thompson Tait—an interest that had faded when he told them what had just happened.

On the short drive over from Kace's he had called Rick to let him know what happened and to warn him about possible attacks from Serge. Rick was infuriated and promised to take Serge down—and until he did, to provide some protection for Sawyer and Kace.

"What kind of people are these?" Sheri says. "So dangerous. I just can't believe my Ryan would be mixed up with people like this."

"He wouldn't have to have been for them to have been involved in what happened to him. Could've been wrong place wrong time. Stumbled onto something. Saw or heard something he wasn't supposed to. I'm sure you would've mentioned it," Sawyer says, "but . . . the masked guy who broke into your house and claimed to be Ryan . . . he didn't have an accent, did he?"

She looks up and closes her eyes as if attempting to access her memory. Twisting her lips and frowning in concentration, she eventually shrugs. "I'm not sure. I . . . I guess it's possible. He was whispering and I was so scared that all I could hear clearly was my heart thumping in my ears. But . . . there could've been a slight one . . . that may be why I knew it wasn't my Ryan. I'm just not sure."

Sawyer nods. "It's okay. I just wondered if it might be Serge, but . . . it's hard to see why he would. Actually, I'm having a hard time seeing why anyone would do that. What was the point?"

"Exactly," Robin says. "Makes no sense. But you don't have to worry about that anymore. Let the police figure it out and deal with it."

When Sheri opens her eyes, she looks at Robin.

"You okay?" Robin asks her.

She shrugs again. "Okay enough."

Speaking with Sheri now makes Sawyer wonder if he can continue working the case quietly, in the background, without Serge knowing he's doing it.

I've just been too out front, too careless. What if I take a lower profile approach? Is it worth the risk? Could I do it and keep Kace, Mom, Sheri, and Addie out of it?

Sawyer looks at Sheri. "Before I quit completely . . ." he says, "I'd like to do a few more things—very low-key in the background in such a way that Serge would never know. I really want to talk to Tad, Jennifer, and Amy. They're refusing to talk to anyone—reporters or police—but . . . if you asked them . . . as a personal favor to you . . . if they'd speak to me off the record . . ."

"I can ask," she says. "I think Amy would. Maybe Jennifer, but I doubt Tad would, but . . . all I can do is ask."

"I don't think you should, Sawyer," Robin says. "I think you need to let the police handle it. It's too dangerous. And not just for yourself, but for Kace. How is she?"

"She's shaken up, but she's very tough and resilient. She'll be fine."

"Y'all make such a cute couple," Sheri says.

"They're not a couple," Robin says.

"No, I know. I just mean . . . they're cute. And in those costumes tonight. But, no, I know."

Robin looks at her son. "Is there anything we can do? I know we're a couple of old women, but . . . we're not completely useless. Anything we could do to help make sure Serge doesn't hurt anyone—especially you and Kace."

"I really appreciate it, but . . . I can't think of anything. I don't want anything to happen to you two either."

"We don't either, but . . . we've lived a long time. Most of our life is behind us. If something happened to us . . . wouldn't be nearly as tragic as if something happened to you young people."

"That's so brave and kind of you, but I really think you both need to stay out of it. I'll speak to Amy and Jennifer and then let the authorities deal with it. Hopefully we gave them enough information to help them find out what happened to Ryan and bring down Serge without getting hurt in the process."

"Did y'all get more good information tonight?" Sheri asks.

"Think so. Seems like Sebastian Lewinsky, Hobo Girl's bass player, is the most likely to have been involved. He was the last one to be seen with Ryan and since that night he has exhibited the most suspicious post-offense behaviors."

"The what?"

"The way someone acts following a crime," he says. "The post-offense conduct. The way someone acts can actually suggest guilt. It's often used in court—especially in sentencing—but I'm using it purely psychologically. Observing how people behave following a crime can give us insight into their state of mind. Most people who commit a crime act differently after it. The more significant the crime, the more significant the change in behavior. That's for people with a conscience. For sociopaths, psychopaths, and other such organized nonsocial offenders, the crime can actually become a type of game. These offenders often return to the scene of the crime for the gratification they get out of it, and reach out to either taunt or offer to assist the authorities in the investigation. From a psychological standpoint and post-offense conduct alone, I'd say Sebastian needs to be our prime suspect."

"Not *our*," his mom says. "Not anymore."

"True," he says. "I'm pretty sure Rick agrees and will treat him as such. Some of the other band members may have helped cover it up, or they may have not had any idea what was going on."

Sheri shakes her head and blinks back tears. "I want him to be alive somewhere, but if that's not possible . . . I don't want him to have lost his life over a damn guitar or a stupid barroom brawl. I still just feel like this is all my fault. I should've never left that night or I should've come back when Phil told me how strange Ryan was acting before going out."

"You can't blame yourself," Robin says.

"Well, I do," she says.

"I'm more to blame than you," Robin adds. "I'm the reason you weren't here."

Sawyer says, "It's highly likely that being here wouldn't've changed anything."

"I've never said this to anyone and I really don't want the authorities to know," Sheri says, "but I think Ryan overdid it studying for his exams and all the pressure he put on himself for medical school. I just didn't realize it at the time, but looking back . . . Given the way he was acting, I think maybe he was taking something to keep him from sleeping and to help him focus—and whatever it was coupled with not enough sleep and all the intense stress he was under and then all the drinking that night . . . had him behaving so bizarrely. I don't want anyone to know. I don't want that to be his legacy, but it may have contributed to what happened to him. And as much as I blame myself for what happened . . . I blame Phil even more. I've always felt like he should've stopped him from going out that night, that he should've called me sooner and let me know how exactly Ryan was acting, but he didn't. It was only later that night right before bed when he called to say good night, and even then what he said was vague and didn't come close to telling the real story of how strung out Ryan really was. If he had called me sooner . . . If he had been more accurate in his description, more honest about his concerns . . . I would've jumped in the car and driven back right then."

"He knew that," Robin says. "It's why he wasn't."

"That's why I didn't have a funeral for him—Phil, I mean. Why his grave marker is so small and generic. Plenty of blame and guilt to go around. God, I just want to wake up from this nightmare."

"I was hoping to help find out what really happened," Sawyer says. "Was hoping that would not only give you some peace, but alleviate your guilt. I think you're going to find that there was nothing you could've done to stop what happened— even if you had been here."

"Well, we'll never know now," Sheri says. "And I'm resigned to that fact."

38

Kace is still shaking, her nerves jangling with a raw energy fueled by fear and adrenaline.

She looks down at Charles from where she's pacing not far from the foot of his bed. He's sleeping through this like everything else. Missing so much.

It's probably best.

He'd always been her protector, but even at his strongest and best he couldn't have protected her from someone like Serge.

It was so sweet how Sawyer wanted to—and felt bad because he didn't think he'd be able to. She can't imagine how it must make a man feel to know he couldn't defend the woman he's with or himself. It was so touching for him to say he'd hope that his brief brawl with Serge would give her enough time to run away. It'd probably get him killed, but somehow she knows he would do it.

The threat from Serge has her jumpy and she's seeing Cody everywhere she turns.

Pull it together. You're safe.

She needs to focus on something. Ordinarily that would be the case, but . . .

I can still read about it and look into it in here, can't I? Serge wouldn't know anything about that.

He might. What if your house is bugged?

That's a ridiculous and paranoid thing to say.

She grabs the baby monitor off the nightstand where it is charging and heads to her war room.

I can at least look at the rest of the video footage and see if any of it confirms what Thompson said. And maybe finish looking at the rest to see if anything else stands out. If I find anything I'll turn it over to Rick. Serge'll never know anything about it.

THE BREAKUP BLOG

I have a confession to make.

I cheated on my wife.

You can't imagine how hard that is for me to admit.

And no, it's not what you're thinking. I never had sex with anyone else while we were married. I was faithful to her, to our marriage, to our family, but . . .

The more emotionally unavailable she became, the more emotionally involved with others I became. And not just women. Not just women I found attractive, but guy friends. And not just people, but pursuits—my work, my interests, my hobbies.

I had ongoing and long-term emotional affairs with people and pursuits, and though they never crossed a line that anyone would call infidelity, they took time, attention, energy, interest, and other resources away from my marriage and into other people and things. And it's cheating—cheating in the sense that I cheated her out of certain things that I instead gave to others. Would it have changed anything if I hadn't? I don't think so. I didn't do it until we were really and truly over, even though I still wasn't admitting it. But if I had had more integrity, more honesty, more backbone, I'd have ended our marriage before getting involved in other things and with other people—even if that involvement was mostly only intellectual or emotional.

What if when she pulled away, it was just to see if I'd pursue her again? What if she needed to be needed? What if I could've changed everything if I had just not let my attention wander, not let my interests drift? Maybe I'm to blame for the whole thing? I just might be. And yet, in previous times when she pulled away, when she withdrew, when she closed down, no amount of pursuing or seducing or entreating ever made her open up or come back or become more emotionally available again. So . . . I don't know. If I knew, I wouldn't be writing this damn thing.

39

"Ever been in a relationship where you loved the person more than they loved you?" Amy asks.

Sawyer nods, though he's not sure he ever has.

"It's . . . it can be painful, but mostly it's just there in the background—something you only think about occasionally when something is said or done or not said and not done to remind you."

Amy Wakefield, Ryan's college girlfriend, is a small, sweet, petite kindergarten teacher who dresses nice and smells good. She's got straight blond hair, big blue eyes, pale white skin, and bright red lips. She looks like a modern, cool kindergarten teacher—not the schoolmarms Sawyer had when he was a kid.

She had agreed to speak with Sawyer as a favor to Sheri, but insisted he come to her classroom and said she could only give him a few minutes.

Though there's an underlying and essential sadness to Miss Amy, he doubts that any of her little students ever see it. He's willing to bet that with them she's as effervescent as the bright, bold colors of the letters and images on her many bulletin boards.

"Ryan and I had a trip planned for that Monday," she says. "Did you know that?"

He nods again.

"Even though he had disappeared and wasn't responding to calls or texts, I still showed up at the airport, bags packed, ready to go on our adventure, hoping against every voice inside my head that said he wouldn't be there, that he wasn't just missing but was already dead. I waited and waited—long after we missed our flight, long after Philip and Sheri tried to get me to leave. God, they were so . . . broken. Just . . . devastated. They knew as well as I did he hadn't just gone off somewhere and lost track of time or was sleeping like a dead man because he hadn't slept the week before. We knew. And still I sat there in that little airport until it closed. Didn't know what else to do."

"I'm so sorry."

She dabs at the corners of her eyes with a small pink tissue, sniffles, and clears her throat.

"Sorry to bring up such painful memories," he says.

"It's always with me," she says. "Always. I'm sure you've heard all the people in the true crime community speculating he was going to propose to me on our trip to Miami. Well, he wasn't. He had no interest in getting married. I'm not saying I was a placeholder girl exactly, but . . . he was never going to marry me and we both knew it. It's amazing all the things people theorize without any evidence or proof at all."

"I know."

"Some of them also say I had something to do with it," she says. "They see that footage of him talking to those girls outside a few minutes before the bar closed and . . . think I killed him in a fit of jealous rage or something. Doesn't matter that I wasn't here. I knew Ryan slept around some. Did I want him to? No. Of course not. But I knew that was part of the . . . price, I guess, that I paid to be with him. He didn't do it a lot. But he was always looking. He was always horny as hell and he was a big, good-looking guy. He never had to look far. Between us . . . I'd be surprised if what happened to him didn't involve a girl. But I never got jealous. He never denied me . . . anything. Never neglected me. And when I was around he was with me—not anyone else, not even looking. It was just when we were apart."

Sawyer nods and wonders if that's really the case or a pristine version of it.

"Do you know that I kept calling and texting his phone?" she asks. "Every day. Without fail. Left messages until I filled his inbox and couldn't leave any more. Called and called and called."

Ryan had still been on his parents' plan and Sheri kept paying the bill hoping he might answer someday or that the authorities might be able to check his phone.

"In all that time he only picked up once," she says. "Well, not him, but whoever has his phone. It was on his birthday, which . . . I don't know . . . makes me think whoever killed him knows when his birthday is, but . . . why answer it and not say anything? Could've just been a coincidence, but it's hard to believe it was. "

He thinks about what that might mean. Is it possible Ryan's still alive? Did he start to answer her in a moment of weakness because it was his birthday? Or is his killer a sadist—enjoying torturing Amy, waiting each day for the phone to ring, the messages to come through? Of course, it could be possible that Ryan is alive but being held captive and his captor wanted to inflict even more pain on his birthday.

"People say I moved on too quickly since I'm with someone else, but I didn't move on for a very long time. At least it felt long to me. And what I did, I did for survival. And between you and me, if by some long shot hail Mary against all odds miracle he showed up alive . . . and would have me back, I'd go back to him in a heartbeat. And I think my Steve knows that. But see, he loves me like I love Ryan. I'm not going to be in a relationship where I'm the one who loved the most again. I can't. It's nice to be on the other side. It's not exactly what I thought it would be, but . . . this is about survival."

"Can you tell me what he said or texted you that night?" Sawyer asks. "Was any of it suspicious? When you look back on it now, does anything seem to have a different meaning?"

"It was pretty much the usual stuff," she says. "Anytime he was out drinking and I wasn't with him he'd get super horny and sweet. He'd call just to say he wished I was there, or that he wanted me, or would I please jump in the car and come join him. Stuff like that. The longer the night went on . . . the more explicitly sexual he'd get."

"Did you ever go and meet him?"

She nods. "A few times. Depending on how far away I was and how early in the evening he started asking me to. I'm . . . a bit of a people pleaser in general, but when it came to him . . . I had a hard time saying no to anything he wanted."

Sawyer starts to say something but she continues.

"He said if he ever even thought about going out with Tad again to slap the shit out of him and remind him of what a douche he is. He said Jennifer was okay, but he hated the way Tad treated her. I suspect . . . he either had a thing for Jennifer or they had slept together at some point in the past. I don't know that, but I think most of his and Tad's arguments were over girls—even when they both had girlfriends."

"How intoxicated would you say he was?"

"Extremely," she says. "Even for him. I'd say he was on something besides booze too. He didn't really do drugs—except when he was prepping for projects or studying for exams. I don't think he had slept more than a few hours in a week. And the later it got, the worse he got. Slurring his words. Being loud and belligerent. Not making sense. One of the last things he said to me was something about being a better guitarist than the guy in the band and maybe takin' his job. Showin' Tad . . . something, maybe that he wasn't a joke or something like that. Didn't even say he loved me when he hung up—and he always did that. The very last time I heard his voice, his last words to me ever and they were a garbled, muddled mess."

40

"**D**oesn't matter who asks," Jennifer Oliver is saying, "Tad won't talk to you. Nothing personal. He won't talk to anyone. He's even stopped talking to me."

Jennifer Oliver, Tad Roberts former sometime hookup, is the only female beautician at an old-fashioned barber shop.

"Why do you think that is?" Sawyer asks. "What's he hiding?"

"Why's he have to be hiding something? What if he told all he knows when it happened and doesn't know anything else? Should he just keep sayin' the same thing over and over or start making shit up?"

"I don't think those are the only options. Most people know more than they think they do and being asked different questions by different people can sometimes help bring it out."

"Or make them make shit up," she says. "It's been two years. You forget things. I can't be sure of what's true anymore. You read stuff. You hear stuff. It all runs together. You forget what's what. If I's you . . . I wouldn't believe anything I've got to say."

"Would you be willing to undergo hypnotherapy?" he asks.

"What? Why? No."

"Everything you saw and heard that night is in your mind," he says. "Hypnosis is a way of accessing it. It can unlock what's hidden away."

"*No way.* Don't want nobody muckin' around in my mind."

"It would be a trained professional who knows what they're doing," he says. "Not a cop or a—"

"No way. No how. Nobody—don't care who it is. Ah man, just thinking about that has me freakin' out. Now I'm stressed as hell. I can't talk about any of this anymore right now. Can we talk more later? Sorry, but . . . I just can't."

41

———

Addie's dad had FaceTimed her and as usual had trashed her mother and promised her everything a little three-and-a-half-year-old girl could want.

She is sad and agitated and Sawyer is trying to think of a way to cheer her up.

He has her by himself—something that happens often, particularly during the day and early evenings when his mom is busy with her active senior lifestyle—the main reason to live in the Estates.

He can't remember if today is dance class and book club or full-body massage and the senior singles interested in other single seniors mixer. He can't keep up. He's just happy she's so active, glad he gets to help her, and pleased that he can keep Addie instead of a babysitter.

"I have a great idea," he says, using the same words and inflection she does when she wants him to do something with her.

She doesn't respond.

"Let's play trick-or-treat."

She looks up at him for the first time, interested, intrigued.

"It'll be good practice for Halloween. You get your jack-o-lantern bucket and I'll get behind a door with some candy."

She bounces up. "Yeah, let's do that."

He quickly grabs her bucket and some random items out of the cabinet, and they rush over to the guest room he's staying in. "Okay, knock on the door and say trick-or-treat."

He enters the room and closes the door.

A moment later he hears a soft little knock that melts his heart.

He slowly opens the door and says, "Happy Halloween."

Her head is back and she is looking up at him with the sweetest, happiest little expression.

"Who do we have here?" he asks.

"It's a little princess," she says, the slightest hint of a lisp melting his heart even more.

She has no costume, but what she has that continues to amaze him is an impressively well-developed imagination.

"What a cute little princess."

Extending her bucket forward, she says, "Happy Halloween. Trick-or-treat. Can I have some candies?"

"You certainly can, Little Princess. Here you go."

He drops a Tootsie Pop, a peppermint, and a package of microwavable popcorn into her little pumpkin bucket.

"Happy Halloween, Little Princess," he says. "Hope you get a lot of candy."

"Happy Halloween," she says. "Now, let's do it again."

"Okay," he says, "I'll close the—"

"Uncle Sawyer, Uncle Sawyer, I've got to pee."

"Okay," he says. "Let's go. I'll race you. On your mark."

She drops her bucket and gets into her little runner's stance.

"Get set," he continues. "Go."

As usual, she wins the race and like always he asks, "How did you get so fast?" as he helps her pull down her pants and panties and sets her on the seat.

She normally says either "I just did" or "At the fast store," but this time she says, "I have fast powers."

"Yes, you do," he says. "The fastest fast powers on the planet."

"We live on planet Earth," she says.

"Yes we do."

"Mars is a planet," she says. "It's hooo-ooot."

"Yes it is."

"I have pee powers too," she says.

"Yes, you do," he says, letting out his delight in amused laughter. "Yes, you do."

42

As Kace sits alone in her war room watching the surveillance footage and making notes, a thought occurs to her. What would happen if they did a reenactment of the night Ryan vanished at Psycho Suzi's with as many of the original players as they could get?

As she's starting to develop the idea and question the safety of something like that given what Serge said, her phone rings.

It's Sawyer.

She hasn't heard from him in a few days and is happy to hear from him. Has missed talking to him, seeing him.

"Hey," she says.

"How are you?" he asks.

"Okay. You?"

"I don't want to do anything to endanger you or Mom or Addie or Sheri," he says, "but I've still been working the case—just trying to do so quietly, under Serge's radar."

"You have? Me too."

"I can't let it go," he says. "I'll wish I had if anybody gets hurt or . . ."

"Same."

"I just spoke to Amy and Jennifer, and I have an idea. What if we see if we can get Suzi to have a Hobo Girl reunion show on Halloween, try to get everybody who was there that night back, and maybe even do a walkthrough of what happened?"

"I was just thinking something similar," she says, "but I didn't think about doing it on Halloween. That's brilliant—if we can pull it off."

"I have some ideas on how we might," he says.

After ending his call with Kace, he calls Rick and pitches the idea to him.

"I like the idea," Rick says. "I do, but it's dangerous . . . Too much liability. Too many things to go wrong. I couldn't . . . I don't know what I'd do if something happened to . . . well, anyone, but especially you or Kace since I recruited y'all."

"I'm not talking about anything official or that you'd be on the hook for," Sawyer says.

"That'd be even more dangerous than if we ran it as an official operation with plenty of help. I'd rather do it that way. Maybe I could call in some favors and get some other agencies involved—maybe even FDLE. Let me think about it and work on it and get back to you."

Later when Sawyer shares the concept with Sheri her face fills with concern.

"I think it's a great idea," she says, "but it's just not worth the risk. I have made peace with everything that happened and with not knowing. If the police find out what happened, fine, but I don't want anything happening to you or your mom or Kace just to give me answers. I just keep thinking . . . knowing what happened to him isn't going to change whatever that was. Isn't going to bring him back to me. It's not worth the risk of anyone else's life. I mean it. I really am at peace now, and part of what helped me get there was Serge threatening y'all. I really, really want y'all to quit investigating. I've come to terms with what having answers is really worth and what it's not. And

it's not worth y'all taking risks like these. It's just not. I'm okay . .
. I really am. And I want y'all to be—you, Kace, and Rick."

"We've been thinking . . . Instead of the request coming
from any of us, it will come from the sheriff's office. Not from
Rick—his name won't even be mentioned—but from the office
itself. I've really thought about it . . . and . . . I wouldn't do it if I
thought it was too much of a risk—especially where you, Mom,
Addie, and Kace are concerned. I don't think it's much of a risk
at all. Kace and I just have to find a way to stay in the background, out of sight, behind the scenes."

"Well, obviously I can't stop you," she says, "but I'd rather
y'all not do it. I have a very bad feeling about it, and the last
time I had a feeling like this and didn't do anything about it, I
lost my son."

43

"Everything is set for the Halloween party at Suzi's," Rick is saying. "She's been extremely helpful and accommodating. The request came from the sheriff's office, so there shouldn't be any blowback on any of us."

Sawyer and Rick are on the way to have one more go at Tad Roberts.

"That's great," Sawyer says. "Thanks for doing it—and for keeping us all out of it."

"Just hope it works and we figure some things out. Oh, and I didn't tell you, but . . . we took it a step further. This is really cool. So . . . we've told everyone—Suzi, the band, the people that were there that night—that this is all part of a true crime TV show and that a camera crew will be there that night filming. Seeing you and Kace use that on Thompson the other night gave me the idea. We're bringing in FDLE agents to pose as the crew. And we've let everyone know about the huge Crime Stoppers reward for anyone providing helpful information. So hopefully they'll be motivated to attend and contribute. And check this—Suzi decided on her own to close the bar that night and make this a private by-invitation-only event. Besides a few of us, everyone there will have been there the night it happened."

"Wow," Sawyer says. "That's incredible. You really took it to the next level."

"I had to do some serious fast-talking to the sheriff, call in every favor I was owed, and if anything goes wrong I'll probably be out of a job, but . . . wanted to roll the dice while we have some momentum on this thing."

"I agree, but it's so brave of you to do. I really admire your approach to your job and appreciate you doing all this. You really think Hobo Girl's gonna show?"

"Oh, yeah, I forgot to mention, I got authorization to use some of the reward money for this event, so we're able to overpay Suzi for hosting the private party and overpay the band reuniting and playing. They'll be there. They're using the lead singer from the band Thompson plays in at the Copacabana. And since it's Halloween she'll be in costume. So for the first time they'll actually have a hobo girl. And, of course, they all think they're going to be on TV."

"That'll bring everyone out in droves."

"I figured we'd also invite people who are connected to the case but who weren't there that night—like Amy Wakefield. I figured you'd be there. Didn't know about Kace. Thought Ryan's mom might want to be. Your mom too, maybe."

Pulling up and parking in front of the Creek County Courthouse, they get out and begin looking for Tad Roberts. Spotting him on the opposite side beneath a palm tree, they head that way.

He's wearing a dark, expensive-looking suit, a white shirt, a burgundy tie, and has a thin briefcase in his right hand. He's talking to what looks to be a colleague—a young woman with short blond hair in a navy-blue pantsuit holding a briefcase of her own.

By the time they reach them, the two are parting company, and as Tad turns he begins shaking his head.

Rick says, "We were hoping that now that you've joined the good guys you might be willing to talk to us."

Tad had recently crossed the aisle and gone from being a high-priced defense attorney to becoming a well-respected prosecutor.

Tad shakes his head and frowns. "It's that kind of thinking that's the problem. There are good guys on both sides. We have to have a good and rigorous defense for our system to work."

"Yeah, yeah," Rick says. "But that's avoiding the question."

"And who is *us*?" Tad asks.

"This is Sawyer Payne," he says. "He's a forensic psychologist consulting on the case."

Sawyer laughs inside—not only at that false description of himself, but at the volume of lies he, Kace, and Rick have told during their short investigation.

"Will you talk to us or not?" Rick asks.

"Have nothing else to add," Tad says. "I've already said all that I know. Don't see the point of saying it again or taking a chance that I might make up something to fill in the gaps of my memory of that night."

Rick starts to say something but Tad continues.

"But I'll tell you this . . . Ryan wasn't the saint everybody's trying to make him out to be, and I'm not the devil."

"We don't believe either of those things," Sawyer says. "But what specifically do you mean? In what ways was Ryan not a saint?"

"Mostly just women," he says. "He always had a girlfriend. Never knew him without one. But he also was always looking to hook up. I mean always. You should've seen him that night. It was embarrassing . . . Inserting himself into conversations and situations. Drunkenly attempting to flirt."

"Is that what y'all fought over?" Sawyer asks.

"We didn't fight."

"Poor choice of words," Sawyer says. "Sorry. The disagreement you had . . ."

"He was disrespecting Amy even more than usual," he says. "And I didn't like the way he was treating Jennifer. But only a fool tries to reason with someone who's tore up as he was."

"Weren't exactly sober yourself, were you?" Rick says.

"Compared to him I was."

"Did he hit on Jennifer?" Rick asks. "Did it make you mad?"

"I didn't have anything to do with what happened to him that night," Tad says. "Whatever that was. And I have no idea what it was. Don't know any more about it than y'all do—probably less. And I'm not not talking just to be an asshole. I just have nothing else to say."

"I appreciate that," Sawyer says. "But for someone like me . . . new to the case . . . it helps more than you can imagine to hear you say something versus reading it in a report."

"Y'all have any idea how much money I've been offered to tell my story?" Tad says. "I'm not trying to capitalize on this in any way. I wish none of this would've ever happened. It didn't just impact Ryan's life. It's something we all carry. Every new person I meet—every client and coworker—wants to hear about that night. I feel the worst for Amy and Sheri, but it's been unimaginably difficult on all of us. Y'all don't think I want to find out what happened to him more than anybody?"

"You don't act like it," Rick says.

Sawyer can feel himself wince inside, and wishes Rick wouldn't take that tact.

"So because I'm not willing to make shit up and be a part of the circus surrounding this case, I don't want him found?"

"We're not asking you to talk to the media or be a part of anything other than helping us get to the bottom of this thing."

"If I knew anything at all, I would've already told his mom. I just don't."

"Did you actually see him walk over to the band and start talking to them?" Sawyer asks.

"I definitely saw him walk in that direction, but I don't really remember him starting to talk to anybody in the band—but I can't really be sure of that at this point. I just don't remember—and I'm not gonna stand here and make shit up trying to prove to y'all that I'm one of the good guys, trying to be helpful."

"And you didn't notice anybody staring at him, stalking him, getting into an argument with him?" Sawyer says.

"He pissed off a lot of people that night," he says. "Including me. He was acting like he was . . . like he was on something other than alcohol. So there were plenty of people mad at him, but . . . I didn't see anyone who looked like they would kill him over it. But I don't know and I've got to go."

Kace's phone is ringing.

When she looks down and sees it's Sawyer she gets excited, a nervous little jolt of electricity humming through her.

"Hey," she says.

"How are you?" he asks.

"Not bad," she says. "Just bleary-eyed from watching all this surveillance footage."

"Anything . . . interesting?"

"I think so. Be interested to know what you and Rick think. Figured I'd try to get through the rest of it and then have y'all come over and look at everything I find."

"Sounds good. We just spoke with Tad and—"

"He talked to y'all?" she asks, feeling equal parts of excitement and envy.

Why does she have to miss out on everything? Some small part of the child still inside her feels like she's being left out because she's a girl.

"Well, something sort of like it—for a moment at least," he says.

"What'd he say?"

He starts to say something but stops.

"What is it?" she asks.

"Rick thinks he just got a line on Sebastian. I'll call you back in a little while when—"

"You better."

"I will."

"Y'all be careful."

"We will. You too."

She puts down the phone still feeling like she's missing out, sensing self-pity beginning to rise up inside her.

Stop it. Don't you dare give into FOMO. You're better than that. You know better.

She hadn't experienced the fear of missing out in a long time, and she wonders what it means about her emotional state that she is now. Is it an unhealthy obsession with the case—or, even more troubling, with Sawyer? Or is it a healthy desire to live again?

She'll have to give it some thought.

But when she sees the dark figure on the video that might actually be Ryan, she sits up, clicks the mouse to pause the frame, and all thoughts of anything else fade from her mind.

Is that . . .

What she is seeing—or thinks she is—could alter the course of the entire case.

She can't be certain, but a distant shot from an auto parts place not far from Suzi's shows a dark figure walking toward downtown—well after the time Suzi's closed. If she's right and it's Ryan, it means someway, somehow he got out of Suzi's that night without being seen.

Could he still be alive? Did he stage all this to start a new life somewhere? Was he the one who posted on his father's funeral page and broke into his mother's house the other night?

45

———

Jai alai, a variation of basque pelota, is a sport involving a ball that is bounced off a walled-in area with a hand-held narrow wicker basket known as a *cesta*. The sport is mostly played and is most popular in Spain, the south west of France, and Latin American countries.

In the United States, jai alai enjoyed some popularity as a gambling alternative to horse and greyhound racing, and remains popular in parts of Florida, where it's used as a basis for pari-mutuel or pool betting.

Forgotten Coast Jai Alai, North Florida's only jai alai facility, opened in 1978, and from the very beginning was plagued with problems.

Not long before the grand opening, one of the co-owners died of a massive heart attack. His estate, valued at $32 million, was disputed by his heirs, relatives, business associates, and others in multiple court cases that dragged on for more than thirteen years. An attorney involved in one of the cases said, "There are all sorts of wild allegations on the record: suitcases of gems, hidden gold, chicanery, injustice, but nothing was ever proven."

In 1988 the players of Forgotten Coast Jai Alai joined other striking players and walked out over contract disputes. The sport itself was prone to player injuries—cuts and concussions and the like—and of course, the betting component led to increased organized crime activity. However, the decline of the game's popularity in Florida, which began in the 1980s, was mostly the result of changes in state laws and the increased availability of gambling options.

For over three decades, the Forgotten Coast Jai Alai building has been empty, abandoned, experiencing the slow death of decay, the huge facility now known primarily for two things—an enormous infestation of bats and the sometime squat of the mentally ill with nowhere else to go.

As Rick and Sawyer were pulling away from the courthouse, Rick received a call from a narcotics investigator who had gotten a tip from one of his CIs that Sebastian Lewinsky is living rough in the abandoned Forgotten Coast Jai Alai building.

Weeds grow through the cracks in the parking lot and vines cover large swaths of the huge, dilapidated building.

"You're welcome to wait here," Rick says as he puts the car in park. "Or you're welcome to go with me."

"I'd like to go if that's okay with you."

"Sure. Always appreciate having your expertise. Here—" He reaches into the back seat and hands Sawyer a large metal flashlight.

They follow neon graffiti that wraps around the side of the building and into a set of side doors mostly missing the glass that was once in them.

Stepping over and ducking under the shards of glass, they slip into a room of overturned tables and a tile floor covered with betting tickets.

"Want to make a wager?" Sawyer asks.

"On?"

"Whether or not he's in here."

"Should probably make it on whether or not we find him even if he is. This place is bigger than I remember."

Clicking on their flashlights, they pass beneath a bird nest in an exit sign and into a long, dark, narrow corridor.

The foul, feted smell in the air is overwhelming, and Sawyer tries to breathe through his mouth to avoid smelling it.

The corridor is littered with more tickets and trash, an old-fashioned rotary-dial wall phone, and a hand truck. It opens onto a massive lobby with an escalator at one end.

Old windows and holes in the walls and ceiling let a small amount of the late-afternoon sunlight stream into the huge, open area.

Beneath their feet, the soiled carpet is wet and spongey and littered with trash.

Long counters run the length of each wall—one side for concession, the other for betting. An open door behind the betting counter reveals a bank room, its floor littered with empty coin roll wrappers, beyond which is an enormous wall safe.

They maneuver around the charred remains of campfires, broken glass crunching beneath their feet.

On the far wall beyond the escalator, a row of makeshift tents and cardboard houses have been propped up.

"Creek County Sheriff's Investigator," Rick says. "Step out slowly with your hands up and identify yourself."

Two huge black hands slowly poke out from one of the tents.

"Don't shoot damn it. I'm comin' out. Don't shoot me, you son of a bitch."

"I'm not going got shoot you," Rick says. "What's your name?"

"Henry," he says. "Hank."

Henry Hank is a giant with a huge, unkempt fro and a long,

curly black beard, and is in a raincoat and unlaced army boots. And nothing else. The open raincoat reveals a soft, hairy belly, beneath which is a huge unerect phallus hanging to the left.

"Henry Hank is a show-er not a grower," Rick says.

"*Hey*," Henry Hank yells. "Y'all really come here to talk about my big dick?"

"Sorry," Rick says. "But I mean . . . my God. Anyway, we're looking for a guy. Sebastian Lewinsky."

"Seabass, yeah," he says, nodding. "Lives upstairs. But, man, I wouldn't go up there I's you. Bad shit happens up there."

"Anybody else up there?"

"Man, I don't know. Peoples comes and go from this place all the time. I can't keep up. Can I get back to my knitting now?"

"Sure. And thanks for your help."

"Don't mention it. And don't feel bad for gawking at my big donkey dick. Er'body do."

The big man disappears back into the tent that appears far too small to hold him.

Rick moves over to the escalator and Sawyer follows.

Before beginning to climb the steps of the still escalator, he turns and scans the area, his eyes following the moving beam of his flashlight.

"Ready?" he asks.

Sawyer nods.

"I'm going to be looking mostly forward, scanning right and left," Rick says. "Will you keep an eye on what's behind us?"

"Sure."

They begin to slowly climb the metal and rubber stairs, maneuvering around a series of old, large monitors, their glass screens broken, their electronic guts hanging out.

"Creek County Sheriff's Investigator," Rick yells. "We're here to speak with Sebastian Lewinsky. All we want to do is talk to you. You're not in trouble. Not under arrest. Just a quick talk and then we're gone."

As they make their ascent, they begin to hear the enormous cloud of bats from the darkness above, their fluttering wings and the high-pitched chirps and clicks of their echolocation process.

They reach the top floor to find an open space and what was once booze and concession stands. More trash on the floor. More dust on everything. More graffiti on the walls.

Making their way over to the arena, they look in, down the rows and rows of seats to the court below that is littered with trash and containing a single jai alia ball.

Above them the immense black ceiling is moving.

Shining their lights upward they see what appears to be millions of bats blotting out the ceiling.

"That has to be one of the largest colonies of bats in the world," Rick says.

He turns and Sawyer turns with him.

After identifying himself again, he says, "Sebastian? Are you up here? We just want to talk."

There is no answer from the void—only the sounds of bats from the black undulating sea above.

"Doesn't seem like anyone's here," Rick says. "But let's look around a little."

They move behind a concession counter and into a huge commercial kitchen. Most of the appliances have been removed, leaving behind a tangle of exposed wires and pipes.

Sections of the sheetrock walls are missing, revealing the metal frame beneath and the room beyond.

The floors are littered with trash and evidence of campfires and makeshift beds.

More graffiti, thick dust and cobwebs, but also the smell of mildew.

Sawyer senses they're being watched, but when he scans the area with his light no one is there.

Not seeing anyone is not the same as no one being there.

True.

He follows Rick down another corridor, off of which are rooms that look to have once been apartments for players, many of them still containing mattresses—most of which are now on the floor and soiled beyond what it would seem a human being could do.

Occasionally, a bat flutters by them, but for the most part the creatures are not in this part of the building.

Eventually, they arrive back in the second floor lobby close to where they began.

The bats are louder out here, and though most are in the arena, there are plenty out here as well.

They cross the open area, around and in between over-turned tables and chairs, a growing stench assaulting their nostrils.

"Is that—?" Sawyer says.

"Death, yes," Rick says as he withdraws his weapon.

They reach an open elevator shaft on the far wall and look down into its deep, narrow abyss to see several dead bodies in various stages of decay inside.

The sickening smell along with the shock of the horrific sight makes Sawyer dizzy and he nearly pitches forward into the shaft.

Rick grabs him and the two men back away from the terri-fying tableau.

"You okay?" Rick asks.

"Yeah. Sorry about that. Just got light-headed. Thanks for—"

"Don't mention it. Let's get out of here. I'm gonna call for backup and the FDLE crime scene unit. We'll secure the place and start processing the crime scene. If Sebastian is here—"

A dark figure pounces out of the darkness, knocking them down.

Their flashlights fall and roll a few feet away, shining back on them, illuminating a small circle of light on the floor beneath the vast, dark void.

Sawyer turns to see what might be an older, long-haired, long-bearded filthy version of Sebastian Lewinsky on top of Rick.

He pushes up and spins around to help.

At first he thinks Sebastian is punching Rick but then a glint of light reveals he has a blade in his hand and is stabbing Rick repeatedly in a fevered frenzy of surreal proportions.

Sawyer jumps up and kicks the man off of Rick, whose clothes are already wet with blood.

The instant Sebastian hits the floor, he rolls, spins, and turns back toward them, readying himself to lunge back at them to continue his assault.

As he does, Rick, with what seems to be the last remaining life force inside him, raises his weapon and fires two rounds that explode in Sebastian's chest.

The sound is deafening in the darkness and the colony of bats grows louder and begins to swarm around them.

Rick's hand falls to the ground with the gun still in it as Sawyer moves over to him, futilely attempting to stop the bleeding while trying to tap 911 into his phone.

46

"Who the hell are you again?" the sheriff asks.

Sawyer, his hands cuffed behind him, Rick's blood on his clothes, is standing beside the back of the patrol car he has just been pulled from.

It had rained earlier and the air is dense with dampness, the waxed vehicle behind him beaded up with a thousand tiny raindrops.

"Sawyer Payne," he says.

"I know your damn name," Rigsby says. "I want to know just what the hell you were doing here with my investigator and your part in his death."

"He's dead?"

Sheriff Ford Rigsby is both old and old school. Beneath his gray crewcut, his sunburned skin is thick, deeply lined, and leathery. He's a tall, large white man with long arms and thick, scarred hands and misshapen fingers, the joints of which are swollen and deformed.

"Let me explain how this particular type of conversation works," he says. "I'm in charge of the questions. You're in charge of the answers. Stay in your lane and answer my questions. Don't ask me questions of your own."

Sawyer briefly explains his connection to Sheri through his mother and his interest and qualifications for looking into the assault on Sheri and Ryan's disappearance. "I've been unofficially assisting Rick with—"

"Hold on there just a damn minute," Rigsby interrupts. "Unless you want to be charged with his murder and hindering a police investigation, you haven't been assisting anybody in my department, unofficially or otherwise. Understand?"

Sawyer nods.

"I don't know what the hell Carson was thinkin' . . . Guess he wasn't, which is what got him killed, but if I hear you say anything like that again I swear to you I will charge you with his murder—and I can make it stick. Understand?"

Sawyer nods.

"Ask yourself," Rigsby continues, "do you want to go to jail or home tonight?"

Sawyer doesn't have to ask himself the question in order to know the answer.

"And I better not hear that you're investigating our case anymore either," he says. "You're not an investigator. You're not even a forensic psychologist. Yeah, we looked you up. You're an online joke. An internet scammer doling out dumbass dating advice or something. So what if you counseled a couple of cops once. That doesn't qualify you for shit. See him?"

Rigsby points to a casually dressed thirty-something man across the way speaking into a digital recorder.

"He's a reporter," Rigsby continues. "He's also my sister's kid. He'll pretty much print whatever I tell him to. Do you have any idea how much misery I can rain down on you with just one story? Enough to make you wish it had been you instead of Carson."

47

"Are you okay?" Kace asks.

She had hugged him when she first opened her back door to him, and now has smears of Rick's blood on her clothes.

Sawyer shakes his head.

Bleary-eyed and raw-bone weary, he feels depleted in a way he never has before. In every way—emotionally, mentally, spiritually, and physically.

He wishes she were still holding him, wishes he was clean and they were lying down somewhere holding each other.

"I'm sure I'm still in shock," he says, "but I'm not so numb or disassociated that I don't feel anything, because I . . . The guilt and grief are overwhelming."

"What can I do?" she asks.

Hold me some more, he wants to say, but just shakes his head and shrugs.

"I wish there was something I could do," she says. "I feel so bad for you, but I feel inept and ill-equipped for something like this."

He shakes his head. "Don't feel bad. I'm a licensed psychologist and I have no idea what to say or do for someone who just witnessed two people get killed so brutally."

"Who else got killed?" she asks.

"Sebastian," he says. "He was—"

"No, besides him," she says. "You said *two* people."

"Him and Rick."

"When did Rick die?" she asks.

He's confused. "This afternoon," he says. "Not sure exactly when. Had to be sometime between the EMTs arriving and when I spoke to Ford Rigsby."

"No," she says. "Rick's not dead. The news said he's in critical condition following surgery, but he's not dead."

Had Rigsby meant he was as good as dead or was he lying to him to increase and intensify the threats he was making against him?

"I realize the outlook's not too good, but he's still alive, which means he at least has some slim chance of survival."

"The sheriff told me he was dead," he says. "Said he could charge me as an accessory to his murder."

"Oh my God," she says. "You . . . poor—come here."

She steps toward him and hugs him again.

"To go through what you went through and then to be threatened with something like that . . . It's . . . criminal."

"Maybe I am responsible in some way for what happened to Rick," he says. "If I hadn't been there—"

"He would've bled to death long before someone eventually found him," she says, stepping back and making intense eye contact with him. "You saved his life—knocking Sebastian off him. Calling an ambulance. Applying pressure to his wounds until the EMTs got there. Every second of life he's fortunate enough to get . . . is because of you."

"That's—"

"It's true," she says. "Positively and absolutely."

He frowns and shrugs, wishing she was still holding him.

"Hey," she says, "I've got something that'll make you feel better. I've been watching the surveillance footage and—"

"Kace," he says. "I can't. We've got to stop."

"But tomorrow is Halloween," she says. "It's now or never. This is what we've been waiting for. I think I've discovered footage from inside Suzi's that has been altered and maybe even a shot of Ryan actually outside of the bar later that night. It's an image caught by a security camera from the parts place on the corner."

"It's too risky," he says. "We've got to stop. We've been . . . People are getting killed. And think about it . . . If Rigsby catches me working on the case he'll bury me—in the legal system *and* the media. And if Serge Birkin finds out, he will bury *us*—literally. We can't keep . . . I can't believe you would even want to. Besides, we now know it was Lewinsky. Hopefully even with him dead they can trace his known whereabouts from back then and find Ryan's remains. Hell, they're probably in that elevator shaft."

48

____

"Play with me," Addie says.

She has followed him into his room repeating her most oft heard mantra—the one he has always responded to in the past in the affirmative.

"I can't right now, baby. I'm sorry. I'm not feeling—"

"I'm not a baby. Play with me."

"Uncle Sawyer's not feeling too good right now," Robin says, coming up behind her. "Let's give him a few minutes to himself."

"NO," she yells. "I want to play with Uncle Sawyer."

He adores her and loves that she likes playing with him so much. He plays with her in a way no one else in her life does— with focused, active attention and imagination. Usually he is powerless to refuse her, but at the moment he has absolutely nothing to give.

"Please be a big girl for me," Robin says. "Sheri and I'll play with you. And we'll have some popcorn and chocolate milk. Come on."

"NO. I don't want popcorn and chockee milk. I WANT Uncle Sawyer."

"I'll play with you in a little while," Sawyer says. "Let me get cleaned up and then—"

"Get your pineapples," she says.

This is her way of saying she wants to get in the shower with him. The bathing suit he wears when she gets in the shower or bath with him has pineapples on an orange background on it.

"I've got something icky on me," he says. "Let me wash it off and then you can get in with me. Okay? Go play with Nana for a little while and then you can join me. Okay?"

Sheri appears at the door behind them. "Come on, Addie. I'm making popcorn. Let's eat some with some chocolate milk."

"NO. I want to play with Uncle Sawyer."

Robin picks her up and begins carrying her out. Addie screams and flails and Sawyer is afraid she might fall. Somehow Robin prevails and they leave the room, Sheri shutting the door behind them.

Having her carried out like that hurts his heart so deeply he can actually feel it—even in his current uncomfortably numb state.

He takes a moment. Takes a deep breath. Then he begins undressing, throwing his clothes in the trash can instead of the laundry hamper.

He feels bad for Rick. He feels bad for how he left things with Kace. He feels bad for not being able to play with Addie. But mostly he feels nothing.

After undressing, he stands there naked, needing to shower, for the moment unable to move.

Eventually, when he can move, he takes the most immediate irresponsible and self-destructive action he can. He texts Jules.

What are you doing?

When he doesn't get an immediate response, he drops his phone on the bed and stumbles to the shower.

Making the water as hot as he can stand it, he barely notices the sting on his reddening skin as it sluices down his weary body.

He thinks about what happened, the events replaying in his mind as if witnessed by someone else.

He feels disassociated, far away from everything—even his own thoughts.

While in custody, he heard the sheriff and other investigators talking about Lewinsky.

He had experienced a psychotic break and the onset of schizophrenia sometime near when Ryan disappeared. After being diagnosed and undergoing some inpatient treatment, he had broken out of the facility and disappeared. Off his meds since then, he had been living rough and evidently growing increasingly violent. They theorized that Ryan may have been his first victim but wasn't his last.

Sawyer stays in the shower until all the hot water is gone. And then for a while after that, barely noticing the icy needles poking into the blood-reddened surface of his canned-ham skin.

When he finally gets out of the shower, he towels off only slightly and falls into the bed still damp, lacking the energy and the will to do anything—even get under the covers.

A faint hum and muted ringing in his ears feels like the aural equivalent of the psychological shock he's experiencing.

His phone vibrates from somewhere on the bed, and without moving anything but his arm, he feels for it.

When he finds it and slides it up to somewhere close to his face, he sees that he has a text from Jules.

Not much at the moment. You? Wanna come over?

Given what he's gone through today, he wants to be held, wants badly to connect to another human being—physically, emotionally, maybe even sexually—but knows Jules is the last person on the planet he needs to seek those forms of comfort from.

Good decision, he thinks. *Don't make things worse by trying to get something you need from someone who has proven over and over she doesn't have it to give.*

I do, he texts. *On my way. Be naked when I get there.*

49

Kace knows Sawyer has been through a lot. She can't really even imagine going through what he just did. But she's disappointed at how he reacted and can't help but feel like he's giving up.

She doesn't think the case is over. Obviously it's not. Far too many unanswered questions.

She wants to know exactly what happened to Ryan—even if Sebastian Lewinsky is responsible for it.

But what if he's not?

What if his psychotic break has nothing to do with Ryan's disappearance? It's possible. They at least have to consider that. They've got to be willing to explore everything. What if his break is related to Ryan's disappearance—but only indirectly? He could've witnessed something rather than done it.

She's hoping Sawyer is just in shock and will come back around, but they're running out of time. Tomorrow is Halloween and she thinks there's little chance of him snapping out of his funk before then.

No matter. She doesn't care what he does, she's not about to give up or give in. How can she?

She doesn't care about Serge Birkin's threats or anything else. His threats are no worse than Cody's were. Maybe it's because she doesn't really have a life anymore that she's not so concerned about the possibility of giving it up, but whatever the case may be, she can't quit.

She wonders with Rick in the hospital if the other cops will still be at the Halloween party at Suzi's, and decides she's going whether they are or not.

With all the original people there on Halloween, she can't help but feel that more facts will come out, more truths revealed, more suspects identified, more insights gained—and she's not about to let that opportunity pass her by. She can't imagine waiting another year to have this chance again, and she knows this particular opportunity—a closed party at Suzi's with the people who were there that night and Hobo Girl playing—will never happen again.

50

———

She meets him at the door in a pair of well-worn jeans and a simple baby-blue tee that shows off the curve of her shapely, small breasts and the outline of her nipples.

She is barefooted and her nails are painted a deep, dark red just like he likes them.

He's instantly aroused.

She shakes her head.

"I just want to talk," she says. "I don't want to have sex. And I don't want any love talk. It's too confusing for me. Gets my head all . . ."

He nods and though they both know he doesn't mean it, she steps aside and lets him in.

When she has closed the door and turns, he is there.

He takes her in his arms, hugging and holding her, her body relaxing into and responding to his.

Eventually, his hands reach her face and he holds her head as he kisses her.

She shakes her head. "No," she says, but it's obvious she doesn't mean it. "Let's just talk."

"You never want to talk," he says.

She feels so familiar and yet even thinner, if that's possible.

The smell of her hair and neck and breath send him.

"I want you," he says.

"You just want sex."

"I want sex with you. Only you."

Even as he says it he thinks of Kace.

She's not an option.

Would you be here if she were?

Put her out of your mind.

"I want you," he says. "You. I want to be inside you."

What he's saying is true in this moment. Totally and completely true.

He knows what she likes, what gets her going, and he does those and only those things.

"Please," she says. "Please stop."

He does.

They're both breathing heavily and take a moment to slow both their heart rates and breaths.

Taking a step back, he says, "Sorry. I shouldn't have . . . I . . . Can we sit on the couch? Could I have some water?"

She nods.

He stumbles over to the couch and she steps into the kitchen.

As far as he can tell, she has yet to change a single thing about their apartment—including the various pictures of them in happier times that are scattered throughout.

There are nearly as many pictures of them as there are of Ryan in Sheri's house.

He knows he'll never been able to tell Sheri what happened to her son, and it makes him feel like a failure, suffuses his heart with a not unfamiliar melancholy.

He also knows in this moment that he could, with relative ease, talk Jules into getting back together.

It would end his banishment from his job, from his old life. It would solve so many problems, and yet . . . he recalls how closed she is, how unwilling to open up or deal with her issues or work on their relationship. And as her frequent criticisms echo through his mind, he knows they made the right decision —even with what it has cost him.

They made the right decision, and as she comes out of the kitchen without the glass of water, disrobing as she approaches him, he knows they're about to make a wrong one.

THE BREAKUP BLOG

I got involved with someone who admitted she was dead inside, who was closed off, and had both daddy and trust issues. And I knew it. And that's on me. I went in with eyes more or less wide open.

I was going to be the miracle worker who brought her back to life. She had closed herself off to everything. Attempting to experience less pain, she experienced less joy. That was the tradeoff and she was okay with it.

And it wasn't just that I saw all the warning signs. She pointed them out. She hated her mother, had conflicted relationships with everyone in her family. She had been the baby for so long, but then her parents had had twins later in life—a boy and a girl that she despised because they took her place.

Her dad had violated her trust over and over—breaking promises and failing to provide her with emotional or financial security, and she had decided a long time ago to never trust anyone again. And foolishly I thought I could change all that. I could be the difference maker for her. Long before my publisher got a ridiculous domain for me about how I was a kind of hero of love, I was already attempting to be—at least for her. I'm as ridiculous as my publisher—more so.

She was sexually closed off as well. But did I let that stop me? Of course not. She had been raped by two boys she went to high school with and had had a very conflicted and fraught relationship with sex ever since, often vacillating between hyper-sexual and asexual. But, of course, I was going to show her how safe she could really be, how gentle and caring a good man could actually be, one who loved sex and wanted a lot of it, but was never forceful—and only aggressive when she asked me to be.

I feel like such a failure in so many ways. And I want to say that marrying her was a mistake. And, of course, in one sense it was—in the sense that it didn't last, obviously. But I'm also not completely sure that it was a mistake at all. In some ways I'm proud of myself for taking the risk, for being willing to fail, being willing to be a fool. The thing is, I will be okay. I have the tools to process our breakup— writing this blog is one of them. But her—what about her? Would it have been better for her if we had never gotten together? Did our divorce only confirm for her what she already believed—that she's terrible at relationships and should be single, and love isn't real because it doesn't last, and no one can be trusted, and only fools open up to anyone? I wonder what she would say? Well, I know what she'd say. She wouldn't say anything. So I guess what I'm wondering is what she thinks and feels—even if she can't express it.

I also feel like a failure because I continue to stay in touch with her, continue to see her. Continue to sleep with her. I'm most ashamed about this. It's selfish and I know I've got to stop. But how long will it be before I do?

51

It's late when Sawyer calls Kace—technically already Halloween.

Though she told him and Rick to call anytime, that she rarely sleeps and doesn't mind being awakened from the little light dozing she does, he still feels like a little before two in the morning is pushing it. But he doesn't care. He has to speak to her. He has to apologize for how he acted earlier and try to reconnect with her in some small way.

"Hey," she says, her voice small, dry, sleepy.

"Sorry to call so late."

"Don't be. I'm glad you—"

"I'm sorry for how I acted earlier."

"Are you kidding? You were in shock. And you didn't even do anything all that—"

"I was a pussy—well, a ball sack and I—"

She laughs. "What was it Betty White said?"

"She's the reason I amended my statement."

"'Everybody uses pussy for being weak or soft,'" she says, "'but they should use ball sack instead. Ball sacks are tender and delicate but everyone knows pussies can really take a pounding.'"

He loves that she got and appreciated his reference. Makes him feel even more guilty for what he had just spent the past few hours doing with Jules. And it doesn't help any that at various points throughout it he was thinking of her.

"I was—"

"In shock," she says. "You had just been through the most traumatic event someone can go through. By the way, did you hear the update on Rick?"

"No. What?"

"He's still critical, but he's stable, which is an upgrade. The local news reported that his doctor said if he makes it through the night he has a good chance of making it."

"That's great. I hope he will."

"He will," she says.

Her certainty makes him feel more confident.

"I've been thinking," he says. "If Sebastian is schizophrenic . . . psychotic . . . whatever it is . . . I can't see him being able to make Ryan vanish so thoroughly. I think it would be like his frenzied attack on Rick and he wouldn't care about hiding his body—or even be able to."

"So you're not convinced he killed Ryan?"

"I'm not."

"Me either. Though I will say . . . it's possible he did it. He could've done it before having his psychotic break or . . . what if he killed him and really wasn't concerned about his body not being found, but because of where or how he killed him it worked out that way. He could've killed him next to the bay and rolled his body into it and the bay did the rest. He could've killed him in the construction site and fresh concrete did the rest. Or something else. Again, I'm not saying he did it. I have doubts. I'm just saying him being the killer and Ryan's body never being found could be essentially unrelated."

He loves the way her mind works.

He recalls how little Jules had said when they were together earlier tonight, how she couldn't or wouldn't respond to him on an intellectual or emotional level. His friends called her a dud, saying she had the emotional range of a Daisy Red Ryder BB gun. She had offered him nothing but the physical, the sexual, and he had tried to use that for comfort but it had just made him feel more isolated, sad, alone.

"I want to say again how much I appreciate you and what you bring to this case," he says. "I respect the hell out of your mind and have enjoyed working on this with you more than I can say."

"I feel the same way," she says. "Thank you."

"I've been wondering if they'll still do the party and the operation tonight," he says.

"I don't know. And I'm not sure who to ask."

"I plan to go either way," he says. "But I'll see what I can find out about it in the morning. And I have an idea about how to deal with Serge."

52

As if a replica of that Halloween night two years ago, it's raining—an odd, light rain that refracts the pale, anemic points of light scattered throughout the dark, haunted night in irregular and surreal ways.

More thick mist than light rain, the effect is a hazy, hypnotic vibe, translucent and tremulous.

Suzi's is lit mostly by candelabras and jack-o-lanterns, the flicker of the flames in the darkness creating a strobe-like effect that resembles an early Lumière brothers' short film.

Hobo Girl is playing the Eurythmics' "Here Comes the Rain Again."

Kace is dressed as Cat Woman, the tight leather costume showing just how incredible her figure really is. Though paying homage to the strong, sexy, iconic Cat Women of the silver screen like Michele Pfeiffer, Halle Berry, and Anne Hathaway, Kace's creation is uniquely her own, and though it could be Sawyer's imagination, he believes her movements to be both more feminine and feline than theirs, her attitude more independent and indifferent.

Sawyer is dressed as Woody from Toy Story, which allows

him not only to hide a knife in one of his boots but carry an actual loaded revolver in the holster on his belt. The firearm is a replica of an old cowboy six-shooter and looks like a prop, which is what he's counting on everyone to believe that it is.

Both of them have drinks in hand, but neither of them are drinking—not about to take a chance on being drugged tonight.

As they look around at the crowd, Hobo Girl plays "I'm Only Happy When It Rains" by Garbage, and like with the previous song, it helps to have a female front man, and they've never sounded better.

Scanning the room, Sawyer tries to pick out the undercover police, but is unsure of anyone other than the fake camera crew.

When he sees Serge across the room talking to Suzi, he looks around and locates Deke, his former client and all around dangerous badass with certain sociopathic tendencies. When he catches his eye, he nods toward Serge. Deke smiles and nods.

Serge is dressed as Tony Montana from *Scarface* and Suzi is dressed in drag as Norman Bates in his mother's dress—complete with wig and kitchen knife.

When Serge spots Sawyer and Kace, he leaves Suzi midsentence and heads toward them.

By the time he reaches them, Deke, who is dressed as Denzel Washington's character Eli from *The Book of Eli*, compete with dark shades and a sawed-off shotgun over his shoulder in his backpack, is standing beside them.

As Serge walks up, Kace says, "No, we don't want to say hello to your little friend."

"You guys," Serge says. "What am I gonna do with you? I gave you fair warning, no? I don't get it. Why you not listen to your new pal, Serge, huh?"

"You have time to walk us through your movements on the night of Ryan's disappearance?" Sawyer asks.

Serge stops, shakes his head, and considers Sawyer for a long moment. Laughing, as if genuinely amused, he says, "Okay, cowboy, have it your way. Serge didn't want anything bad to happen to you and your, aw, pussy cat, but . . . What can I do? It's a lesson I have to learn—letting go. I can't take responsibility for other people. Serge must learn this, no? 'God grant me serenity to accept things I cannot change, the courage to change things I can, and the wisdom to know the difference that is between them.' Serge accepts he cannot make you value a long, safe life. I hope you have accepted the fate of the choice you have made."

"Accept this—" Sawyer says. The police are aware of your threats against us and our families. If anything happens to us . . . they would take you down, but—"

"They can't even keep themselves from getting hacked up like Happy Thanksgiving turkey."

"They would take you down," Sawyer says, "if they could, but . . . they won't be able to."

"Exactly," Serge says. "This is exactly right my friend."

"They won't be able to," Sawyer says, "because there won't be anything left to take down. That's because my friend, Deacon Rouse here, will after a particularly brutal and lengthy torture session, obliterate you off the face of the earth as if you had never been born."

Serge looks at Deke for the first time.

At six-six, 260, Deacon Rouse has the hard, muscular body of a professional football player—something that looks even more menacingly cool as Eli.

"The hell are you?" Serge asks him.

"I . . . a sociopath with homicidal tendencies," Deke says in his low, slow growl. "Doc here helpin' me not go around killin' all you rude little bitches that annoy me, but . . . though he has not expressly stated it, I feel confident that he wouldn't mind I made an exception in your case."

There is a palpable change in Serge. He swallows before speaking and his words have the tinny, hollow quality of a bad actor. "If you think Serge can be scared off, man, you—"

"Yeah, yeah," Deke says. "Say your lines so you don't lose face, but . . . we all know you know the real from the fake news. And while we knowin' shit, know this . . . Just in case that little gin-soaked, titty-bar brain of yours thinks sneaking up and back-shooting me will solve your problems, not only do I have eyes in the back of my head, but I have brothers and other family members a hell of a lot meaner than I am that will keep you alive wishing you were dead, begging for your death, a lot longer than I would."

Serge starts to say something, but Deke stops him by holding up his massive mitt of a hand. "Let's be done with this shit," he says. "It beginnin' to weary my black ass and I may have to eighty-six a bitch right here in the middle of this perfect little white people party. Run along now. And from this moment forward, pray to whatever god you pray to that nothin' happens to these two or their families, because if something does—no matter what or who might be responsible—you know what that means for you."

53

"It's so strange to be back," Jennifer is saying. She is one of a handful of people not in costume. "Haven't been since that night."

Kace and Sawyer are standing with Jennifer near the end of the mostly empty bar.

Behind the bar, Suzi is talking to both the bartender and barback, both of whom are older than Kace would expect to see in a place like this—especially the barback, who instead of a kid is a late-twenties man with pale skin, fine blond hair, and blue eyes so light they almost seem colorless.

"Does being here trigger any memories?" Kace asks.

"Sure. Of course."

"Any that you had forgotten about until now?"

She shrugs. "Maybe. I just remember Ryan being so . . . agitated. He couldn't be still. It was like he was hyperactive or something. He kept rubbing and itching his skin like he was having an allergic reaction to something. And . . . he couldn't let anything go. I mean . . . Tad can be a jerk. Trust me I know. But that night . . . Ryan was looking for a fight. Everything bothered him. He took everything the wrong way."

Amy Wakefield, in a small, sexy Little Red Riding Hood costume, rushes over to them.

"I've just remembered something," she says. "I know I wasn't here that night, but . . . somehow it helps to be here. I'm . . . it's unlocking things. I remember this thing Ryan said because that song was playing while we were on the phone."

Kace and Sawyer pause for a moment and look at the band.

Hobo Girl is playing Willie Nelson's "Blue Eyes Crying in the Rain."

"He said a lot of things that didn't make sense that night," she says. "Like I said . . . he was out of it. Exhausted from not sleeping, staying up all week studying, the stress and pressure of his exams. He was strung out on something and drunk. It was hard to hear him when he was in here and he was mumbling and slurring his words. I remember he said something about dropping out of school and joining the band. He was always talking about that—being in a band instead of becoming a doctor. I said something like "You can't do that" or something, and he said, "I may not have choice." I asked what he meant and he just said we'd talk about it later. He hung up a few moments later and I never . . . It was the last time I spoke to him. But . . . something in the way he said he might not have a choice . . . Not sure what that meant, but . . . it sounded like he really believed it—that something he had done or . . . something was going to force him to drop out of medical school."

"And you have no idea what he was talking about?" Kace asks.

"None at all," she says. "Before he always talked about wanting to be in a band. And sometimes he'd say he'd rather do that than be a doctor. Even said he planned to start a band after medical school, but it was always partially playful. And he never mentioned not finishing school—and especially not having a choice about it."

"You can't think of any reason why he'd say something like that?" Sawyer asks. "What he may have meant?"

She shakes her head. "None. Sorry. And it may be nothing, but . . . I don't know. It sounded like something. Anyway . . . just wanted to let you know. I'm gonna walk around some more and see if I remember anything else."

Kace nudges Sawyer with her elbow and points to the door.

He turns to see his mom and Sheri, dressed as two of the Golden Girls, walking into the bar.

Sawyer had explained to them how potentially upsetting and even dangerous it could be here tonight, and they had agreed not to come. They were supposed to have taken Addie trick-or-treating, then to a carnival at the rec center, and yet here they are.

Sawyer starts toward them and Kace follows.

"What're y'all doing here?" he asks when he reaches them.

Sheri shakes her head. "Couldn't stay away. Had to see it all for myself."

"We won't get in the way," Robin says.

"Where is Addie?"

"With the sitter. Told her we wouldn't be long. Y'all just go back to what you were doing. Don't mind us."

"Would y'all like a drink?" Sawyer asks.

They nod and each tell him they'd like a glass of wine and the kind they prefer.

"I'll go grab it. Y'all come on in and find a good spot to sit."

They nod and keep looking around.

"I'll get them situated," Kace says, "while you get their drinks."

Sawyer looks at Sheri. "Is there any reason why Ryan may have had to drop out of school?"

"What do you mean?"

"Did he ever mention anything about not having a choice

about whether he kept attending medical school? Grades? Money? Some kind of trouble?"

She shakes her head. "No. Why? As far as I know everything was fine with school and he was doing well. Surely you don't think what happened to him has anything to do with school, do you?"

54

———————

When Hobo Girl goes on break, dance versions of Halloween music is pumped through the house system.

Sawyer approaches the stage to talk to the band while Kace talks to the two young women who had been seen on the surveillance footage with Ryan outside the bar not long before it closed.

The members of Hobo Girl are dressed as iconic band members—just not the same band. Among them are members of Kiss, the Village People, The Beatles, and The Stones.

"It's so trippy to be back," Terrick Bushnell is saying. Beneath his black rock hair wig, his face is painted white with a black star around his right eye and very red lips. "Never thought we'd play together again—let alone here on *Hallofreakinween*. What the hell, man?"

"Still can't believe that shit about Seabass," Sammy Chastain says. He's dressed as Ringo Starr circa 1969. "It's weird not having him here playing with us."

"What's *weird* . . . is that he lost his freakin' marbles and offed a bunch of people."

Thompson Tait is standing there with them, dressed as the construction worker from the Village People, and appears disinterested and sullen.

Sammy says, "You think if he hadn't killed that Ryan dude and disappeared that night, he might have killed us?"

"I think he may have tried," Terrick says.

"Oh," Thompson says, adding to the conversation for the first time, "'cause you're such a badass and could've—"

"Nah, man, that's not how I meant it. I just meant he might have tried. That's all. Not that we could've stopped him if he did."

"He wasn't a big dude," Thompson says. "Hard time seeing him overpower Shandling."

Sammy says, "All it takes is one surprise blow to the head or stab to a major blood vessel or organ and . . . the biggest, strongest bastard on the planet will be incapacitated."

"Hey, man," Terrick says to Sawyer, "I remembered something while we were playing tonight that I had forgotten. He got into it with the bouncer. Shandling, I mean. He was over by the bar talking to the owner, Suzi, and—it didn't look like a friendly conversation by the way—and the Russian or Ukrainian or whatever he is guy came up and got in his face. Suzi walked away—went into the back I think. Not sure. And Shandling just kind of collapsed onto a barstool."

"I missed all that," Sammy says, "but at one point I saw Jasper try to come around and help him and Serge stop him . . . kind of warn him off."

"Jasper?"

"Tollis. The barback."

Sawyer turns and looks at the almost albino late-twenties barback.

"What happened then?" he asks as he looks back toward them.

"Nothin'," Terrick says. "Was near the end of the night.

Didn't really pay attention to him. Next time he was on my radar is when his drunk ass was stumbling around our equipment."

Thompson says, "Then he made the fatal mistake of following Seabass into the back."

As Sawyer thanks them and moves off to talk to Jasper Tollis, Thompson follows him.

"Hey," he says when they are out of earshot of the other band members. "Them catching Sebastian isn't going to change my TV deal any, is it?"

"It shouldn't," he says. "But it'd help if you think of any other details you can share. I don't mean make anything up. I mean anything you may have held back or anything that you remember because of tonight."

Jasper Tollis's personality is as anemic as his pale appearance.

Though he's in his late twenties, he acts as if he's a prepubescent boy, and implicit in every word and action he takes is an unspoken apology.

"You were working the night Ryan Shandling disappeared, weren't you?" Sawyer asks.

He has been rejoined by Kace. The only thing she had been able to get out of the two young women Ryan had been speaking to out front was that he was most definitely hitting on them and he walked back into the bar as they left.

Tollis nods.

"What were Suzi and Ryan and Serge arguing about?" Sawyer asks.

He shrugs.

"You don't know or you won't say?" Kace asks.

He doesn't respond.

Hobo Girl takes the stage again and opens its next set with "Have You Ever Seen the Rain."

"What made Ryan fall down onto the barstool?" Sawyer asks.

He shrugs again. "Just didn't feel good I guess. I don't know. Everybody always drinks more than they realize. Maybe. I don't know."

"When you tried to check on him or help him, why did Serge stop you?"

"I try to help people," he says. "They come in here for a good time. I just want to make sure they have one and are okay. That's all. But sometimes Mr. Serge has to deal with them his way and it's not my place to do anything. I don't know. I like my job. I like the music and the people having a good time. That's all. I want to keep my job. Don't want to make anybody upset at me. Miss Suzi's so good to me. Like my big sister. Mr. Serge's all right. He just wants people to behave themselves and . . . He's never been bad to me."

"Okay, Jas," Stella, the bartender says, coming up to us. "You're okay. Go get us two more cases of Coors Light."

He nods rapidly and says, "Yes, ma'am."

As he rushes away, Hobo Girl starts "Purple Rain."

Stella is a thin, dark-complected forty-something with long, straight black hair, mesmerizing green eyes, and a mouthful of very white, slightly crooked teeth.

"He's a good kid. Sort of slow and simple, but mostly just shy, quiet, and awkward. Absolute heart of gold. Do anything he can for anybody. Lend them money for more drinks or a cab or even give them a ride home. He gets nervous talking to people—especially when he thinks he might get in trouble for something, so please ask me anything else you want to know."

"He seems so sweet," Kace says. "We were just asking about Ryan Shandling. We were told on the night he disappeared he stumbled onto a barstool and Jasper tried to help him but Serge stopped him."

"Sounds about right," she says, "but I was slammed that entire night and I missed all of it. I'm sure there was nothing to it. Please don't start anything between Serge and Jasper."

"We're not trying to start anything between anyone," Kace says.

"You know what I mean. Don't say anything to Serge or Suzi about it."

"Do you have a theory about where Ryan is?" Sawyer asks her.

"Has to be in here, right?" she says. "I mean, if he didn't leave this place . . . he's got to be in here somewhere."

"You're serious?" Kace asks.

She nods. "It's a big building. There was construction going on. His remains could be in a wall or beneath concrete or in some crawlspace."

"Haven't they all been searched?" Sawyer asks.

She shakes her head. "Not even close. They brought some dogs in and when they didn't find him . . . they sort of assumed he wasn't here. But . . . it's just another case to the officials, right? You need to talk to someone who it's personal for—who searched thoroughly and early on in the process, right?"

"Who would you recommend?"

"A lot of people have searched the place," she says, "but no one any more thoroughly and any earlier than his girlfriend . . . Amy, I think it is. Far as I know she's the only one who searched for him that night."

"Which night?" Sawyer asks.

"Two years ago tonight," she says. "The night it happened. I mean, it wasn't like she was searching for a missing person. She just showed up looking for her boyfriend, but . . . no one else even started looking for him until a few days after that."

55

———

"You didn't tell us you were here the night Ryan went missing," Sawyer says.

Amy looks startled and is unable to speak for a moment. Little Red Riding Hood freezing as if in fear of the Big Bad Wolf. Eventually, she tries to say something, then shakes her head, swallows, and clears her throat. "I wasn't."

"You were seen," Kace says. "We have witnesses."

"I wasn't here when Ryan was here that night," she says. "I wasn't part of anything that went on. I came later. I just . . . I got worried about him. He didn't sound right on the phone and then he stopped answering my calls or responding to my texts. By the time I decided to come check on him it was too late to . . . I didn't get here until after they had closed. There were only a few staff members around, cleaning up, hanging out. They said everyone had already left but I could look around real quick if I wanted to."

"And did you?" Kace asks.

"A little, yeah. Not for long."

"Where all did you look?"

"Everywhere," she says. "Well, everywhere I could. But it was just a quick, cursory glance. I had no idea he was really missing and . . . would never be seen again. I was just making sure my boyfriend was okay. To be honest . . . I figured I'd find him passed out somewhere or having sex with somebody he hooked up with from the bar. I knew they weren't going to let me look for long, so I just sort of ran through everywhere I could."

"Where all did you look?" Kace asks again.

"Everywhere—the construction site, backstage, the elevator, the loading dock. Be easier to tell you where I didn't look."

"Where didn't you look?" Sawyer says.

"I didn't check any kind of attic space or locked storage clos- ets," she says. "And even though I checked the restrooms— male and female—I didn't check every stall. I'm sure I missed other rooms or spaces I don't even know about, but I looked everywhere I could and he wasn't here."

"What time was this?"

"I'm not sure exactly. Probably . . . pushing three. I stopped by the house on the way here. Woke Phil up. Think I scared the life out of him. Always wondered if that contributed to his death . . . If his heart was weak and . . . Did I make it weaker? Anyway, I didn't expect anyone to still be here by the time I got here but there were and they let me look around."

"Who is *they*?" Kace asks.

"Bartender and a waitress," she says. "They're the only people I saw. I heard a few others, but—"

"*Heard*?" Sawyer says. "How? Where?"

"Oh, just in the owner's office," she says. "Backstage. I think that's where they were coming from. There were two locked doors back there. I guess it could've been from either one, but . . . I was told later that one was a storage room, so . . . I was about to knock on both when the bartender appeared at the other end the hallway and said time was up and we had to go. I wish now that I had insisted on seeing who was behind those doors, but . . . like I said . . . at the time I didn't think he was missing— not in the sense that he really was and still is."

56

Approaching Suzi's office, Kace says, "God, I wish Rick was here."

"Yeah, me too. For more reasons than one."

The band sounds different back here—muted as if playing in a mattress factory—but their version of "A Hard Rain's A-Gonna Fall" is unique and interesting, the female vocals inspired.

"You think Serge is in there with her?" she says.

"Should I get Deke to join us?"

"I can't really see a downside to it."

Sawyer pulls out his phone and texts Deke and they continue.

Just before they reach Suzi's office door, it opens.

Serge gives them a big smile and says, "Come on in my fine friends."

They step inside to find Suzi, still in her Norman Bates costume, sitting at her desk, a bottle of Jack and a lowball glass in front of her.

"You saw us approaching because of the security cameras in

the hall," Kace says. "Wonder why they didn't pick up Ryan that night."

Sawyer says, "Witnesses say he followed Sebastian backstage, but he's never seen on the footage. Sebastian is, but not Ryan."

Kace thinks how strange it is that Woody and Cat Woman are questioning Norman Bates while Tony Montana looks on.

"Clearly the crazy man killed him," Serge says.

"Doesn't explain why he's not on the surveillance footage."

Suzi says, "There's a blind spot—the little area right behind the stage and the hallway. Must've done it there."

"So you see, my good friends," Serge says, "the case it is closed. Have a good day. Bye-bye."

"I know you doctored the footage," Kace says. "I've got the clip on my phone. See?" She taps a few buttons on her phone then holds it up. "You have to really be looking for it. It's good work, but it's there. Just the faintest flicker where empty hallway footage was inserted over the footage of Ryan back here. The question is . . . Why would you do that? Surely you wouldn't doctor the footage to protect Sebastian, would you? You have no loyalty to him, do you? I guess you could've done it to protect your business—remove the footage of Sebastian killing Ryan for the sake of your business, but . . . My guess is you did it for the only reason you would do—to protect yourself."

"When Ryan came back here it wasn't to talk guitars with Sebastian," Sawyer says. "He came to see you."

Suzi lets out a laugh, but it sounds forced and hollow. "You see a little static on your phone and you start accusing me of . . . what exactly? That's slander and I can sue your ass."

Her empty threat is made all the more absurd by the costume she is wearing.

Sawyer says, "Y'all argued out in the bar and he came back here to finish it."

"You can call it static on my phone if you want to," Kace says, "but I've watched it a few dozen times on a huge high-contrast monitor and it's an edit, not static or a glitch. There's another one a little later too. You covered up what happened in that hallway, but it doesn't matter what I see. It matters what the FLDE crime lab tech sees."

"What were you arguing about?" Sawyer asks.

"Listen to me, my man," Serge says. "There was no argument. The guy was trashed. Wasted. Not making any sense."

"Tell you what," Sawyer says, "you tell us what he said and we'll decide for ourselves if it makes sense or not."

"Tell *you* what," he says, "I'll shoot you in the face and you decide if it hurts or not."

"Brilliant way to convince us y'all had nothing to do with Ryan's disappearance," Kace says.

"And genius move given all the cops around," Sawyer says.

Suzi nods toward the monitor hanging on the wall across from her desk. They turn to see Deacon Rouse approaching the office door, his weapon drawn and down by his side.

"Jesus, man," Serge says, "but that's a big bastard." He turns back to Suzi. "You want I should pop them all?"

"No, of course not," she says, shaking her head.

On the monitor, Deke can be seen standing to the side of the door, his weapon up and ready. The sound of the knock arrives a split second before the monitor shows him knocking.

"I'm not gonna have a shootout at my place of business," Suzi says. She looks up at Sawyer. "Call your man and tell him to holster his weapon and stand down. Tell him we're about to open the door very slowly and Serge is going to join him in the hallway while the three of us talk for a minute."

He does. As soon as Deke has his weapon holstered, Sawyer opens the door.

"Everything's fine here," Suzi says. "I'm going to talk to these two while you two wait in the hallway—with your mouths shut and your guns holstered. I mean it. I don't want a scene of any kind. Understand? All we'll be doing in here is talking. All you'll being doing out there is waiting—silently. Understand?"

When the two men are in the hallway and door closes behind them, Suzi says, "If I can prove to you that I had nothing to do with Ryan's disappearance, would you agree not to involve the police?"

If Kace is right and the figure she saw on the security footage from the store on the corner is Ryan, then Suzi didn't have anything to do with what happened to him, but she wants to know what the woman knows, wants to hear what she has to say.

She nods.

"I want to hear you say it," Suzi says. "Both of you."

They verbalize it.

"I'm gonna tell you the truth," she says. "The business I'm in . . . the things I do . . . a person is nothing without her word. I'm giving you my word that I'll tell you the whole truth, and you're giving me your word that if I had nothing to do with what happened to him, you'll drop this here and now—my part of this—and not mention it to anyone, including the police."

"We are," Kace says. "I give you my word."

"But is your word any good? Is his? Thing is, all I could get popped for on this is withholding evidence in an investigation, so it's no big deal, but I don't want the cops tramping through my business with their big black boots."

"Our word is good," Sawyer says. "I guarantee that. I'm a counselor who never reveals his clients' secrets. She's a nurse who never reveals her patients' problems. We keep our word. We would've been out of business long ago if we didn't."

"Anyway . . . so here it is. God as my witness. You're right about Ryan coming back here and me taking that part out of the video. Thing is . . . Ryan and I had a little history. Few times over the years . . . if his horny ass couldn't find someone to go home with—or in the back alley with—he'd come up here and see me. He was a pretty good kid. Had a killer body. So . . . He'd finish too fast, but he'd be ready to go again pretty soon afterwards. 'Course he'd finish too fast again then, but . . . he'd mostly do what I told him to. Wasn't a regular thing or nothin', but it was fun when it happened. He . . . used to confide in me. I was like a surrogate big sister or something. And when he needed something to help him stay awake to study or whatever, I'd get it for him. That night he was wired and exhausted and just out of sorts. He called me over there by the bar and said he had seen Jasper, my barback, slip something in a few of the guys' drinks. Said he was watching him because he felt funny and he thought someone had put something in his drink."

"That little prick is who drugged me," Kace says.

"He tried to drug Sammy and got you by mistake," Sawyer says.

"I told Ryan to settle down and I'd take care of it," Suzi says.

"Didn't exactly do that, did you?" Kace says. "Two years later and the little creep is still doing it."

"I'm amending our agreement," Sawyer says. "Turn Tollis in and terminate him immediately—something you should've done years ago."

"I'm supposed to care if some privileged, entitled, rape-y fraternity boys get a little dose of their own medicine?"

"Actually, you are," he says. "But I don't have time to teach you how to be human being right now, so just say you'll fire and report him."

"I'll consider it," she says. "Can we get back to that night? Ryan tried to get belligerent but got dizzy instead and had to sit down. I walked away from it. Don't know what happened after that. Not much, I'm pretty sure. Anyway, when he knocked on my door later, he was really out of it. He wanted to give it a go, but he was in no condition, so I let him lie down on the couch for a while. That's it. I didn't—we didn't have sex or anything."

"Doesn't explain the blood in the back of the hallway," Sawyer says.

"Seabass had a nosebleed," she says. "Had nothing to do with Ryan. It looked like Ryan was following him backstage, but he wasn't. Once back here, Ryan came to my office. And Seabass—after doing some crazy shit with his equipment— had one hell of a wicked nosebleed. I'm tellin' you he was already losin' his shit that night. All that business with the equipment . . . I guarantee he thought it had been bugged by the government or something like that."

Sawyer nods. "Makes sense."

"And I ain't even got no big-time degree or student loans," she says. "Anyway, later that night when he was ready to leave, I let him. I figured he was just going to walk home. Had no idea something would happen to him and it would turn into all this."

"He left from the side door, didn't he?" Kace says.

She nods.

"The camera footage captures the door closing," Kace says. "Doesn't show anything else."

"Yeah," Suzi says. "It shows if someone walks in but not if they walk out, unless they pause in the doorway for some reason."

Kace turns to Sawyer. "I keep telling you the footage is the key to solving the case. I know Seabastian was losing his shit that night and much of what he did with the equipment was strange, but I bet it looked even more bizarre because of what she edited out to hide Ryan's presence back here. And if I'm right about that one shot from the corner store being Ryan . . . it confirms what she's saying."

Sawyer looks back at Suzi. "Is that why you used that door, to hide the fact that he had been back here with you?"

"What? *No.* I wasn't trying to hide him. I hadn't done anything wrong and I couldn't know that something was going to happen to him. It was just bad luck that it happened that way."

"Was this before or after his girlfriend came looking for him?" Sawyer asks.

"After. Why?"

"Because that means she could have still been out looking for him when he left."

57

By the time Kace and Sawyer get back out into the bar area, the party is breaking up. The band has stopped playing and is tearing down and most of the people have left or are in the process of leaving.

Scanning the room for Amy and not finding her, they rush down the stairs and out into the parking lot.

The parking lot is busy and full, people in various stages of loading up and pulling out.

The rain has stopped, but every surface is still wet, glistening with refracted light.

A flash of red on the far west end and they are rushing toward Little Red Riding Hood.

"Hey there, Little Red Riding Hood!" Sawyer shouts.

When she doesn't turn, Kace yells, "AMY."

She turns to see them and stops getting into her car.

"What's wrong?" she asks when they reach her. "What is it?"

"Where did you go when you left the bar that night?" Sawyer asks.

"That's why you chased me down out here—to ask me that?

I went home. I figured Sawyer was somewhere with someone and he'd call me the next morning. Why?"

"You didn't see him that night?"

"*What*? NO. Why—what makes you . . . You know I didn't."

"We don't know anything," Kace says. "We didn't know you were here that night."

"I told you," she says. "I wasn't. Not until after everyone was gone and then only for a few minutes. And then I drove home."

"You drove all the way here, looked around for a few minutes, and then drove back home? You expect us to believe that?"

"I don't expect you to do anything," she says. "I'm just answering your questions. Why are you asking them?"

"Can anyone verify what time you got home that night?"

"Yeah," she says, nodding, but doesn't offer any more.

"Who?" Sawyer asks.

"My roommate. She was a sorter for UPS and was always up getting ready for work around that time. I've really got to go. Can you tell me what this is about?"

"As soon as we know, we'll let you know," Kace says. "We're just trying to exhaust all possibilities."

"Well, I think you've done that where I'm concerned. Definitely exhausted the hell out of me."

58

"I was hoping we'd find out tonight," Kace is saying. "I just thought if we got everyone together in the same place on the same night . . . I guess my naïveté knows no bounds."

On their walk home, they are going by the spot where someone was caught on the security camera of the store on the corner—the footage she finally got Sawyer to look at, though on her phone instead of her large monitor.

Beneath their feet, the damp pavement shimmers, reflecting the pale illumination of both moon and manmade lights.

"We found out a lot," Sawyer says.

"Yeah, a whole lot of who *didn't* do it."

"Which puts us closer to knowing who *did*."

"I don't think it does," she says. "I think it puts us right back to square one."

She wonders how odd it must look for Woody and Cat Woman to be walking and talking their way through the empty streets of this old North Florida port town.

"At least we now know he got out of the bar and how," he says.

She wonders if he really feels as positive as he's projecting or if he's doing it for her benefit. Either way it's sweet, if a little Pollyannaish.

"Which means he could be anywhere," she says. "I really don't think I'm cut out for this shit. I'm too impatient. Want to know what really happened too bad. And I want to know right now. I can't begin to see how Rick has lived with this for two years now."

"I hope he lives with it many more years to come."

"You don't think we're going to solve it?"

"I just meant I want him—"

"I know and I do too. I'd give up solving the case to have him back working on it. But I'd like to have both—him back and we find Ryan and give his mom some peace or something."

Sawyer says, "I don't think cases like this get solved."

She stops and looks at him, considering him for a long moment, twisting her lips, frowning, and nodding. "I haven't wanted to admit that to myself, but the moment you said it some part of me knew it was true."

"Sorry," he says. "I don't want it to be true."

She nods and starts walking again.

"Here we are," she says, pointing up to a security camera on an automotive parts place at the corner of an intersection about a block from Psycho Suzi's. "Why in the hell would he come this way? It's the opposite way from home. If it was him, where was he going? Was he turned around? Confused? Going to meet someone?"

"That's what we've got to find out," he says. "And we will."

She shakes her head. "I don't think we will. I think we've come to the end of what we can find out from an investigative standpoint. I've gone over all the video. If it's even him in the footage from here—and it may not be, probably isn't—the trail goes cold here. There's nothing else. I mean nothing. I think we've exhausted everything from an investigative and forensic approach—there's a reason why this case is so cold two years later. I had hoped you could figure something out from a psychological perspective, but..."

"That was way too much to hope for from Your Love Guru dot com," he says.

59

For the rest of the walk back to her place, he goes over every facet of the case again, attempting to apply psychological principles, questioning everyone's behavior and actions, trying to suss out motivations and the type of poker-like tells that might give away a killer.

As they near her house she breaks the silence by asking, "What are we missing?"

He smiles.

"I know, I know," she says. "If we knew that, we wouldn't be missing it."

He stops walking and turns toward her.

"I want to say something," he says, "and there's nothing behind it, and I hope you won't find it offensive, but . . . you are hands down the coolest, prettiest, sexiest Cat Woman ever—and that's saying something, given the incredible women who have donned that iconic outfit."

She is visibly taken aback. "Wow. Thank you."

Suddenly, the moment becomes fraught, filled with an intensity he hadn't intended, and he takes a few steps away from her, attempting to diffuse it, glancing over at Sheri's house as he does.

"That means more than I can . . ." she adds, and then as if trying to dampen down the electricity arcing between them says, "Especially coming from such a smart, handsome Sheriff Woody."

"Well, good night," he says. "And Happy Halloween. Sorry we got more tricks than treats, but . . . there's always next year."

She shakes her head. "I can't put in another year on this case. I just can't. The not-knowing is driving me—"

Not knowing . . .

Sawyer doesn't hear the rest of what she says, because in that moment he knows what happened to Ryan.

Who is the not knowing not bothering like it should? Whose post-offense behavior indicates both knowledge of the crime and guilt from being involved in it? Who is not as frightened as they should be?

Who is most likely to have done it, now that we know Ryan actually left the bar that night?

60

"Figured I'd find you here," Sawyer says.

She turns from Ryan's final resting place and considers him, and he can tell she suspects he knows.

"It's a lovely grave marker," he says.

She nods.

"Phil killed him, didn't he?" Sawyer asks.

She reacts as if having been punched in the stomach, her surprised expression confirming the truth of what he has said.

She nods, resignation replacing the surprise on her face.

"He didn't mean to," Sheri says. "It was all a horrible accident."

He has found her in her garden on this anniversary of the night of her son's death. She has long since taken off her costume. She is not a character, but a grieving, broken mother. This is not a holiday but a holy day.

"He never would tell me all the details," she continues, "just that Ryan was really strung out and aggressive and they started fussing and then fighting. He didn't mean to kill him. He just tried to survive and subdue him. Ryan's head got bashed in by that damn stone monstrosity of a fireplace I had to have. If I had been here . . . I could've . . . It wouldn't've happened. But you know where I was—a stupid Halloween party out of town. When I got back the next day, Phil had already buried him back here in the garden. Said he didn't want anyone seeing Ryan like that or knowing he had attacked his own father. Was probably more to it than that. I'm sure some self-preservation or panic took over too. What he did was stupid beyond all—but I believed him that it was an accident and he was at least in part trying to protect me from seeing Ryan like that and trying to protect Ryan's reputation. We could've never guessed it would turn into this world-wide unsolved mystery phenomenon, but when it did I couldn't very well reveal what really happened and be able to prevent it from becoming the biggest circus on the planet."

"I'm so sorry for your loss," he says. "For all you've been through—and all that comes with the intense media and true crime community interest."

She nods and thanks him. "How did you figure it out?"

"Just began to apply post-offense behavior to everyone instead of just Sebastian. Thought about how Phil acted both before and after Ryan's disappearance. How you acted toward Phil—while he was alive and since his death. How you've treated this place—how much time and care you lavish on this garden while Phil's generic little headstone is neglected and covered with weeds. The picture of Ryan, the one in the costume he wore that night—the last one he ever took from the day of his death, the one you cropped Phil out of—hanging above that missing chunk of stone on the fireplace. Your unwillingness to sell, your fight with the Estates about your garden and the golf course. How you weren't really afraid of being here because there was no break-in. You staged that yourself. The figure was tall and thin—like you. I remember thinking if it was Ryan he had lost a lot of weight since he went missing. You hid the costume, which I assume was over your pajamas then broke the glass out of the door as we were running around to the back. There was no break-in, just a break-out. That's why no one was around. There wasn't time for your attacker to disappear that quickly. Then you ran and jumped in bed. That's why your face was so red and you were so out of breath. I thought it was because you were upset by the attack. At some point later you hid the costume in the sand trap. No one had a motive for doing that, for pretending to be Ryan and telling you he's okay, except you. But I'm still not sure why you did it."

"Me either," she says. "It was so stupid. I didn't think it through. Just thought it would throw some confusion into the mix, maybe get some people to thinking he was still alive, so they wouldn't look too closely at me and Phil. It was . . . just a dumb, dumb thing I did."

"Did you post the message from Ryan on Phil's memorial guestbook?"

She nods. "Another moment of brilliance on my part," she says, shaking her head and letting out a harsh little laugh. "Did some research online on how to do it. Put on a disguise and went to an internet cafe and . . . Anyway . . . What else gave me away?"

"How at peace you've been with supposedly not knowing what really happened to Ryan. Not knowing what happened to Ryan is disturbing Kace far more than you—and the only way that can be is that you don't not-know, but know. You were absolutely fine with us stopping the investigation once Serge threatened us. You were fine because you already knew. You had been humoring us throughout because you already knew what really happened. Phil killed Ryan. And you killed Phil."

"Well, I guess I did, but not really," she says. "I was so . . . livid. I believed him. I knew how Ryan could get when he was on drugs and alcohol after a week of no sleep, but . . . I just couldn't forgive him—even for an accident. Couldn't let it go. It just festered inside of me, grew into this huge black thing eating my insides out. We were in the attic getting the Christmas decorations down—something I did not feel like or want to be doing—and I just lost it. All I did was charge him and shove him. That's it. He fell backwards, tripped on one of the exposed trusses and fell through the ceiling onto the floor in the hallway. It knocked the breath out of him but he seemed fine. Not that I cared. I didn't. He went to the hospital to get checked out and when they asked what happed he just told them he stumbled and fell through. When he came home he acted like nothing had happened. Didn't even mention it. And neither did I. I knew I owed him an apology, but I just couldn't . . . Three days later, he was dead. Delayed aortic dissection. They say the trauma from the fall caused a small, pain-free tear in his aorta. They probably would've seen it if they had done an MRI, but when the chest X-ray was normal they didn't do anything else. So, yes, I guess I killed him—at least the action I took led to his death, but when I lost it and shoved him it wasn't with the intention of killing him. Who would ever think shoving someone would kill them?"

"Does Mom know?" he asks.

She shakes her head. "Only two people on the planet know —and they're both here right now."

He nods and thinks about it, and they are quiet a few moments.

"What are you going to do?" she asks.

"What do you mean?"

"Now that you know," she says.

"Oh," he says. "Nothing."

"You're not going to tell anyone?"

He shakes his head. "There's only two people I want to tell —just for their sake. Rick and Kace. I know I can't tell Rick because of the position it would put him in and what he'd have to do about it. But Kace . . . I think she will keep our secret. I really do, but I'm . . . It's not me who would be at risk if for some reason she didn't, so . . ."

"Tell the poor dear," she says. "I've started to more than once. She's got an unbelievably difficult life and she has invested so much in trying to bring me closure. She won't tell anyone. And, Sawyer, thank you. Thank you for your understanding and kindness. And for calling it our secret."

61

"That'll be two dollars, sir," Addie is saying.

She has just made Sawyer a pretend cup of coffee.

They are out in the front yard in the late afternoon of a pleasant and picturesque North Florida November day.

He pays her with his pretend money and takes his cup of coffee.

"Thank you, brother," she says. "Come again to see us."

She's heard someone—most likely on a TV show—call someone *brother*, and she's been using it a lot, saying it with perfect attitude and diction. She got her version of *come back to see us* from him when their roles were reversed and he was the barista.

"Have a good day," he says.

"Have a good day, brother," she says.

"Thank you, brother," he says.

"No, I'm a sister."

"Oh, sorry. Have a good day, my sister."

An elderly couple in tennis attire drive by in a golf cart and wave and say, "Hey Addie."

"Someone just *hey*ed me," she says.

"They sure did. Everyone here adores you. But no one more than me. You're such a smart and fun and funny and loving little girl. I'm so proud of you. And I love your imagination."

As if not hearing any of that, she says, "Okay, you be the coffee person now and I'll be the . . ."

"Customer," he says.

"Yeah."

"Okay," he says. "Hi, ma'am, welcome to Uncle Sawyer's Grind House. What can I get started for you?"

"I would like a coffee please, sir," she says. "Thank you, brother."

Robin emerges from the front door with a folding chair and joins them in the yard.

"Nana, you want some coffee?" Addie asks.

"I'd love some."

"Okay," she says. "I will fix you a cup."

She takes the cup and maker from Sawyer and begins to earnestly prepare her grandmother a fresh cup.

"How are you?" Robin asks her son in the way only a mother can.

He looks up at her, squinting a bit at the low afternoon sun behind her. "I'm okay."

"I know y'all were hoping to solve the case on Halloween, but . . ."

"Yeah, but it's okay. I've sort of let it all go for now."

He had come close to confiding in his mother a few different times, but had ultimately decided not to. No need to burden her or her friendship with Sheri with such things. He is still undecided about whether he'll tell Kace that he solved the case and won their bet, but he's leaning toward it.

"It's been good for you to do that," she says. "I can tell."

He nods. "It has. More time with you and Addie. More time to work through some things related to Jules and our . . ."

She nods.

They are quiet a moment, listening to Addie talk to herself as she makes the coffee.

"I know you're going through a difficult time and the circumstances aren't ideal," his mom says, "but I've got to say . . . it has been so nice having you here. And you're changing that little girl's life."

"Thank you so much for letting me stay here and for making me feel so welcome. Being here has done me more good than I can say. And *this* girl . . ."

"Hey, sister," Addie says to her grandmother, "your coffee's ready, ma'am."

"Thank you, ma'am."

"That'll be ten dollars," Addie says, holding out her little hand.

"Coffee's gone up," Sawyer says.

"Still a bargain," Robin says, pulling actual money from her pocket and giving it to Addie.

"*Oh wow*," she exclaims as she takes the real dollar bills.

"If it's okay with you I'd like to stay a little longer," he says.

"Stay forever," she says. "Or at least until you meet one of these rich old ladies around here to marry."

62

A few days later, as Sawyer walks her to her door, Kace can tell he has something he wants to tell her.

They have just returned from the hospital after visiting Rick, who, though he has a lot of healing and rehab in front of him, is going to make it, and may even be back at work before Christmas.

And that's not the only good news she's received lately. All indications are that Charles is improving and may once again be going into remission.

She wonders if what Sawyer has to say is related to that. He seemed so genuinely happy for her—for them both—but there is an undeniable attraction between them, and they've shared many moments of intimacy that have been intense and erotically charged. Is he about to tell her that they need to stop working together, hanging out, seeing each other? God, she hopes not. That would break her heart. He's the centerpiece of what little bit of life she gets to live.

"I'm so glad we went to see him," he says. "Seemed to really do him good. Thanks again for going. I realize how difficult it is for you to get away, but I knew he would want to see you."

"I was so happy to get to go. It does me more good than I can say to get out occasionally."

"And again, I'm so happy for your good news about Charles."

"Thank you."

He turns to leave and she tries to think of something to say to keep him a moment longer.

"Hey," she says.

He stops and turns back to her.

"Do you think what Suzi said about Sebastian could be true? That he did all those things with the equipment because he was having a psychotic break?"

He nods. "It's certainly possible. I've seen several cases where the person's paranoia has them believing things of theirs are wired by the government to spy on them—refrigerators, receptacles, blow-dryers, car headlamps. We'll probably never know for sure, but that would certainly explain it."

"Why do you think Serge warned us off if they didn't have anything to do with Ryan's disappearance?"

"Well, they did have *something* to do with it—and he may have thought Suzi had more than she did, but I suspect it's because of all their other criminal activities. But who knows what motivates a man like him?"

"You're supposed to," she says with a smile.

"Abnormal psyche doesn't get that abnormal."

She wants to ask him if he's the person writing the Breakup Blog, but can't bring herself to do it, so instead says, "Did you hear that Jasper Tollis was arrested?"

"I did," he says. "Made me exceedingly happy."

"Should we tell Rick what we know about Suzi and Serge, their businesses, their involvement in what happened to Ryan?"

"We gave our word we wouldn't," he says. "I think we have to honor that. Besides, he probably knows most of it. Knowing it and being able to prove in court are two very different things."

She knows that. She just wanted to keep him here longer. She doesn't say anything else right away, and a moment of awkward silence passes between them.

"I . . . I felt like you had something you wanted to tell me," she says.

"Oh," he says. "Nothing that can't wait. You're dealing with enough right now."

"Okay, but I really, really like dealing with our stuff and anything that's not related to running my little one-patient hospital."

He nods. "Good to know."

When he turns to leave again she says, "Are we still going to work this case?"

He stops and turns again. "I thought from what you said the other night that you really didn't want to keep—"

"I was just tired and frustrated," she says.

"I get it," he says, nodding. "Well, then, let's continue when you have time."

"I have time," she says. "I have so much time."

"Then," he says, turning to leave again, "Cat Woman and Sheriff Woody are back on the case."

She watches him walk away for a moment longer than she should, then turns and goes inside, closing the door behind her and leaning against it for a moment, taking a deep breath and transitioning back into nurse-wife mode.

As she does, a stack of mail on the foyer table catches her eye and she steps over to it.

Junk. Junk. Bill. Bill. Magazine. Amazon package . . . And then she sees it.

At a single, split-second glance she recognizes his handwriting.

Her response is instant and visceral, fear firing in every synapsis, humming along every live wire nerve.

The plain brown envelope has nothing but her name on it. No postage means he had hand delivered it to her box—unless he's been inside her house. Either way he's been here and knows where she lives.

Shaking so badly she has a hard time opening it, she rips both the envelope and the single sheet of matching stationary inside.

On the thin, small piece of paper that flutters to the floor as she snatches back from it, letting go of both it and the envelop as if poison, are only four little words—words that depending on the context could be seen as sweet and romantic, words that in this context are creepy and threatening and menacing.

Four words he's said to her before.

Four words burrowed into her brain so deeply and with such trauma that they can never be exorcised.

Four little, innocuous words, each a separate sentence.

Every. Breath. You. Take.

MORE GREAT BOOKS

Go to www.MichaelLister.com for more great mysteries and thrillers.

All of Michael Lister's books are available in hardcover, paperback, ebook, and audiobook.

Join Michael's VIP Reader's Group today for free books, news, reviews, recommendations, and content you can't get anywhere else.